"How did you know I was going over there to...to try to..."

"Cassie, honey, you call me, ask if I'd settle in here for the night because you need to see Devin—I'm going to figure it out," Edwina Crump said straightforwardly. "And it's long past time, if you ask me."

Cassie looked down at her plain cotton blouse and simple trousers. "Ed, I'm no good at this sort of thing."

"I'd wager Devin's plenty good at it, so don't you worry."

"Maybe I should put on a dress," Cassie fretted.

"Cassie." Ed peered over her rhinestone glasses. "He doesn't care what you're wearing, take my word for it. Now go get him."

"All right." Cassie squared her shoulders. "I'm going."

Poor kid, Ed thought. She looked as if she was walking out in front of a firing squad. With a cackle, Ed turned back to the TV.

Her money was on Devin MacKade.

Dear Reader,

Once again, we've got an irresistible month of reading coming your way. One look at our lead title will be all you need to know what I'm talking about. Of course I'm referring to *The Heart of Devin MacKade,* by award-winning, *New York Times* bestselling author Nora Roberts. This is the third installment of her family-oriented miniseries, "The MacKade Brothers," which moves back and forth between Silhouette Intimate Moments and Silhouette Special Edition. Enjoy every word of it!

Next up, begin a new miniseries from another award winner, Justine Davis. "Trinity Street West" leads off with the story of Quisto Romero in *Lover Under Cover.* You'll remember Quisto from *One Last Chance,* and you'll be glad to know that not only does he find a love of his own this time around, he introduces you to a whole cast of characters to follow through the rest of this terrific series. Two more miniseries are represented this month, as well: *The Quiet One* is the latest in Alicia Scott's "The Guiness Gang," while Cathryn Clare's "Assignment: Romance" begins with *The Wedding Assignment.* And don't forget Lee Magner's *Dangerous* and Sally Tyler Hayes' *Homecoming,* which round out the month with more of the compellingly emotional stories you've come to expect from us.

Enjoy them all—and come back next month for more excitingly romantic reading, here at Silhouette Intimate Moments.

Yours,

Leslie Wainger
Senior Editor and Editorial Coordinator

Please address questions and book requests to:
Silhouette Reader Service
U.S.: 3010 Walden Ave., P.O. Box 1325, Buffalo, NY 14269
Canadian: P.O. Box 609, Fort Erie, Ont. L2A 5X3

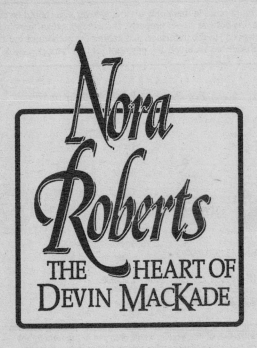

Nora Roberts

THE HEART OF DEVIN MacKADE

Silhouette®
INTIMATE™MOMENTS®

Published by Silhouette Books

America's Publisher of Contemporary Romance

For those who follow their hearts

 SILHOUETTE BOOKS

ISBN 0-373-07697-5

THE HEART OF DEVIN MACKADE

Printed in U.S.A.

Dear Reader,

What could be more intriguing than one not-quite-reformed bad boy? How about four of them? That was one of the seeds that grew in my mind to form The MacKade Brothers. I very much enjoy writing connecting books, particularly when they center on families. And, well, I just like men. I've been surrounded and outnumbered by them all my life. I'm the youngest of five children, and the only girl. I have two sons, and no daughters. Though the male of the species isn't easy to understand, I think those facts give me a leg up. So I decided to write about four brothers, four men who had been just a little wild in their youth.

I enjoyed the challenge of exploring the dynamics of this, and in putting those four men in a small town where everyone knows everyone else, and all their faults and virtues. I created the town of Antietam, though it's not so very different from the small towns near where I live in Maryland. I created the MacKades, though I like to think they're not so different from men who live and love anywhere in the world. Though I started off with Rafe— because he struck me as the baddest of the bad MacKade Brothers—I fell in love with Jared, then with Devin, then with Shane.

If a woman's still breathing, she'll fall for the MacKades. Rafe, the businessman, with a dream and an attitude. Jared, the lawyer, with a reputation and a surplus of pride. Devin, the lawman, who believes in justice and abiding love. And Shane, the farmer, with the love for the land and an eye for the ladies.

I hope you'll enjoy all of their stories. And if you fall a little bit in love with each of these not quite reformed bad boys, don't worry. You're only human.

Nora Roberts

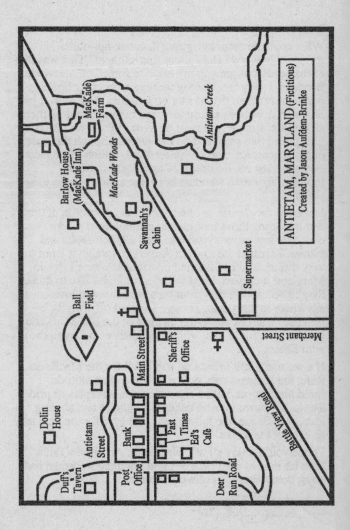

ANTIETAM, MARYLAND (Fictitious)
Created by Jason Aufdem-Brinke

Antietam Creek

MacKade Farm

Barlow House (MacKade Inn)

MacKade Woods

Savannah's Cabin

Supermarket

Ball Field

Main Street

Sheriff's Office

Merchant Street

Dolin House

Antietam Street

Bank

Past Times

Ed's Café

Duff's Tavern

Post Office

Deer Run Road

Battle View Road

Prologue

Devin MacKade considered the age of twenty to be an awkward time in the life of a man. It was old enough for him to be considered responsible for actions and deeds, old enough for him to make a living or love a woman. Yet in the eyes of the law it was not quite old enough for him to be considered fully adult.

He was glad it would only take twelve months to get through it.

Being the third of four brothers, he'd already watched Jared and Rafe move beyond him into adulthood, and Shane was not far behind him. It wasn't that he was in a hurry, really. He was enjoying his time and his life, but Devin had begun, in his methodical way, to make plans for what would be.

The little town of Antietam, Maryland, would have

been surprised to know that he had decided to uphold the law, rather than break it. Or bend it.

His mother had pushed him into college, true, but once he arrived, Devin had decided to enjoy it. The courses in administration of justice, criminology, sociology, fascinated him. How rules were made, why, how they were upheld. It had seemed almost from the beginning that those books, those words, those ideals, had just been waiting for him to discover them.

So, in his thoughtful way, he had decided to become a cop.

It wasn't something he wanted to share with his family just yet. His brothers would rag him, undoubtedly. Even Jared, who was already on his way to becoming a lawyer, would show no mercy. It wasn't something he minded. Devin knew he could hold his own with all three of his brothers, be it with words or fists. But for now, it was a personal agenda, and he wasn't talking.

He was aware that not everything you wanted, deep inside, worked out. There was proof of that right here in Ed's Café where he and his brothers were grabbing a quick meal before heading to Duff's Tavern to shoot pool. Yes, the proof was right here, serving him the blue plate special, flushing shyly at Rafe's easy teasing.

Five foot two, barely a hundred pounds, as delicate and fragile as a rosebud. Angel hair like a curling halo around a face that was all quiet gray eyes. A nose that tipped up just the tiniest bit at the end. The prettiest mouth in the county, with its deep dip in the top lip. Like a doll's. Small hands that he knew could juggle plates and coffeepots and glasses with a studied competence.

Hands that carried a ring with a chip of a diamond barely big enough to glint on the third finger.

Her name was Cassandra Connor, and it seemed he'd loved her forever. Surely he'd known her forever, watched her grow up with a flicker of interest that had become a full-blown crush he'd considered too embarrassing to act on.

And that was the problem. By the time he decided to act, he'd been too late. Joe Dolin had already claimed her. They would be married in June, just two weeks after she graduated from high school.

And there was nothing he could do about it.

He made sure not to watch her walk away from their booth. His brothers had sharp eyes and he would never be able to tolerate being teased about something as intimate and humiliating as unrequited love.

So he looked out the window at Main Street. That, he thought, was something he could do something about. One day he would give something back to the town that had been such an intricate and important part of his life. One day he would serve and protect here. It was his destiny. He could feel it.

The way he sometimes felt, in dreams, that he had done so before—or tried, when the town was ravaged by war, split and frayed by divided loyalties. In dreams, he could see it the way it had been, the way it was in those old Civil War photos. Stone houses and churches, horses and carriages. Sometimes he could almost hear the men gathering on corners or in the barbershop, discussing the War between the States.

Of course, he thought with cool rationality, the town, or parts of it, were haunted. The old Barlow place on the hill just outside of town, the woods, his own home, the fields he helped plow and plant every spring. There were echoes there of lives and deaths, of hopes and fears.

A man had only to listen to hear.

"Almost as good as Mom's." Shane shoveled mashed potatoes into his mouth, and the MacKade dimple flashed as he grinned. "Almost. What do you figure women do on their night out?"

"Gossip." His plate clean, Rafe leaned back and lit a cigarette. "What else?"

"Mom's entitled," Jared commented.

"Didn't say she wasn't. Old lady Metz is probably giving her an earful about us right now, though." Rafe grinned wickedly at that thought, and at the knowledge that his mother could handle even the formidable Mrs. Metz with one arm tied behind her back.

Devin looked away from his view of Main Street, back at his brother. "We do anything lately?"

They all thought about it. It wasn't that their memories were poor, it was just that they found trouble so easily, they often overlooked the results.

Anyone breezing by the big window of Ed's Café would have seen the four MacKades, dark-haired, green-eyed devils, handsome enough to raise any female's blood pressure, be she ten or eighty. Reckless enough to have most men bracing or backing away.

They argued awhile over who had done what most recently—fights picked and fought, laws broken, or at least dented. It was agreed, after the argument grew heated, that Rafe had the prize, with his race against Joe Dolin's Chevy on route 34.

They hadn't been caught, but word had gotten around. Especially as Rafe had won and Joe had slunk off muttering about revenge.

"The guy's a jerk." Rafe blew out smoke. No one disagreed, but Rafe's gaze shifted to where Cassie was busy serving a booth behind them. "What does a sweet little thing like Cassie see in him?"

"If you ask me, she wants out of the house." Jared pushed his plate aside. "Her mother would be enough to send anyone looking for the first escape hatch. The woman's a fanatic."

"Maybe she loves him," Devin said quietly.

Rafe's opinion of that was one crude word. "Kid's barely seventeen," he pointed out. "She'll fall in love a dozen times."

"Not everyone has a flexible heart."

"A flexible heart." Shane whooped with laughter at the phrase. "It ain't Rafe's heart that flexible, Dev, it's his—"

"Shut up, creep," Rafe said mildly as his elbow jammed hard into Shane's ribs. "You up for a beer, Jare?"

"I'm up for it."

Rafe leered nastily. "Too bad you two have to stick with soda pop. I bet Duff has a whole case of the fizzy stuff for you kids."

That, of course, insulted Shane. As it was meant to. Hot words came first, then the jostling. From her station at the counter, Edwina Crump shouted at them to take it outside.

They did, with Devin lagging behind to pay the tab.

On the other side of the window, his brothers pushed and shoved each other, more out of habit than from any real temper. Ignoring them, he smiled over at Cassie.

"Just blowing off steam," he told her, adding a tip that wouldn't embarrass her.

"The sheriff sometimes comes by about this time of night." Her voice was barely a whisper of warning. And so sweet to Devin's ears, he almost sighed.

"I'll go break it up."

He slid out of the booth. He thought his mother probably knew his feelings. It was impossible to hide anything from her. God knew, they had all tried and failed. He thought he knew what she would say to him.

That he was young yet, and there would be other girls, other women, other loves. She would mean the best by it.

Devin knew that though he wasn't yet be fully an adult, he had a man's heart. And he'd already given it.

He kept that heart out of his eyes, though, because he would hate Cassie's pity. Casually he walked out of the diner to break up his brothers. He caught Shane in a headlock, elbowed Rafe in the gut, cocked a brow at Jared and suggested amiably that they go play some pool.

Chapter 1

The town of Antietam was a pretty sight in late spring. Sheriff Devin MacKade liked to walk the uneven sidewalks and smell the freshly mowed grass, the flowers, hear the yip of dogs and shouts of children.

He liked to take in the order of it, the continuity, and the little changes. Outside the bank, a bed of pink begonias was spreading. The three cars jockeying in line at the drive-in window constituted a traffic jam.

Down a little ways, in front of the post office, there were men passing the time, taking the air. Through the barbershop window, he could see a toddler experiencing his first haircut, while his mother bit her nails and blinked damp eyes.

The banners were flying for the annual Memorial Day parade and picnic. He could see several people busily scrubbing or painting their porches in preparation for the event.

It was an event he enjoyed, even with its logistical and traffic headaches. He liked the continuity of it, the predictability. The way people would plant themselves with their folding chairs and coolers along the curb, hours before parade time, to ensure that they would have a good view of the marching bands and twirling batons.

Most of all, he liked the way the townspeople threw themselves into that weekend, how much they cared, how strong their pride.

His father had told him of the ancient man who, when he himself was a little boy, had walked creakily down Main Street wearing Confederate gray at an earlier Memorial Day. One of the last living testaments to the Civil War.

Dead now, as they all were, Devin mused as he glanced over at the memorial in the town's square. Dead, but not and never forgotten. At least not in little towns such as these, which had once known the sound of mortar and rifle fire and the terrible cries of the wounded.

Turning away, he looked down the street and sighed. There was Mrs. Metz's Buick, parked, as usual, in the red zone. He could give her a ticket, Devin mused, and she would pay it. But when she lumbered into his office to hand over the fine, she would also treat him to a lecture. He blew out a breath, studied the door of the library. No doubt that was where she was, gossiping over the counter with Sarah Jane Poffenberger.

Devin drew together his courage and fortitude and climbed the old stone steps.

She was exactly where he'd expected her to be, leaning over the counter, a mountain of paperback novels at her dimpled elbow, deep into the latest dirt with the librarian. Devin wondered why any woman so... generously sized insisted on wearing wildly patterned dresses.

"Mrs. Metz." He kept his voice low. He'd been tossed out of the library many times in his youth by Miss Sarah Jane.

"Well, hello there, Devin." Beaming a smile, Mrs. Metz turned to him. Her elbow nearly toppled the mountain of books, but Miss Sarah Jane, for all her resemblance to an understuffed scarecrow, moved fast. "And how are you on this beautiful afternoon?"

"I'm just fine. Hello, Miss Sarah Jane."

"Devin." Iron gray hair pulled back from paper-thin white skin, starched collar buttoned firmly to her chin, Sarah Jane nodded regally. "Did you come in to return that copy of *The Red Badge of Courage?*"

"No, ma'am." He very nearly flushed. He'd lost the damn book twenty years before, he'd paid for it, he'd even swept the library for a month as penance for his carelessness. Now, though he was a man—one who wore a badge and was considered responsible by most—he was shriveled down to a boy by Sarah Jane Poffenberger's steely eyes.

"A book is a treasure," she said, as she always did.

"Yes, ma'am. Ah, Mrs. Metz..." More to save himself now than to uphold parking laws, he shifted his gaze. "You're parked illegally. Again."

"I am?" All innocence, she fluttered at him. "Why, I don't know how that happened, Devin. I would have sworn I pulled into the right place. I just came in to check out a few books. I'd have walked, but I had to run into the city, and stopped by on my way home. Reading's one of God's gifts, isn't it, Sarah Jane?"

"It is indeed." Though her mouth remained solemn, the dark eyes in Sarah Jane's wrinkled face were laughing. Devin had to concentrate on not shuffling his feet.

"You're in the red zone, Mrs. Metz."

"Oh, dear. You didn't give me a ticket, did you?"

"Not yet," Devin muttered.

"Because Mr. Metz gets all huffy when I get a ticket. And I've only been here for a minute or two, isn't that right, Sarah Jane."

"Just a minute or two," Sarah Jane confirmed, but she winked at Devin.

"If you'd move your car—"

"I'll do that. I surely will. Just as soon as I check out these books. I don't know what I'd do if I didn't have my books, what with the way Mr. Metz watches the TV. You check these out for me, Sarah Jane, while Devin tells us how his family's doing."

He knew when he was outgunned. After all, he was a cop. "They're fine."

"And those sweet little babies. Imagine two of your brothers having babies within months of each other. I just have to get over to see them all."

"The babies are fine, too." He softened at the thought of them. "Growing."

"Oh, they do grow, don't they, Sarah Jane? Grow like weeds, before you can stop them. Now you've got yourself a nephew and a niece."

"Two nephews and a niece," Devin reminded her, adding Jared's wife Savannah's son, Bryan.

"Yes, indeed. Give you any ideas about starting your own brood?"

Her eyes were glittering at the thought of getting the inside story on future events. Devin stood his ground. "Being an uncle suits me." Without a qualm, he tossed his sister-in-law to the wolves. "Regan has little Nate with her at the shop today. I saw him a couple hours ago.

"Does she?"

"She mentioned Savannah might be coming by, with Layla."

"Oh, my! Well..." Being able to corner both MacKade women, and their babies, was such a coup, Mrs. Metz nearly trembled with the idea. "Hurry on up there, Sarah Jane. I've got errands to run."

"Hold your horses now, I've got 'em for you right here." Sarah Jane handed over the canvas bag Mrs. Metz had brought it, now pregnant with books. Moments later, when Mrs. Metz puffed her way out, Sarah Jane smiled. "You're a smart boy, Devin. Always were."

"If Regan finds out I headed her over there, she'll skin me." He grinned. "But a man's gotta do what a man's gotta do. Nice seeing you, Miss Sarah Jane."

"You find that copy of *The Red Badge of Courage*, Devin MacKade. Books aren't meant to be wasted."

He winced as he opened the door. "Yes, ma'am."

For all her bulk, Mrs. Metz moved quickly. She was already pulling out of the red zone and into the sparse traffic. Congratulating himself on a job well done, Devin told himself he could take a quick ride down to the MacKade Inn.

Just needed to check and make sure there wasn't anything that needed his attention, he told himself as he walked up the street to his cruiser. It was his brother Rafe's place, after all. It was his duty to check on it now and again.

The fact that Cassie Dolin managed the bed-and-breakfast and lived on the third floor with her two children had nothing to do with it.

He was just doing his job.

Which was, he thought as he slipped behind the wheel of his car, a huge and ridiculous lie.

He was, however, doing what he had to do. Which was to see her. At least once a day, he simply had to see her. He just had to, no matter how much it hurt, or how careful he had to be. More careful, he reminded himself, now that she was divorced from that bastard who had beaten and abused her for years.

Joe Dolin was in prison, Devin thought with grim satisfaction as he headed out of town. And he would be there for quite some time to come.

As the sheriff, as a friend, as the man who had loved her most of his life, Devin had a duty to see that Cassie and the kids were safe and happy.

And maybe today he could make her smile, all the way to her big gray eyes.

What had been the old Barlow place—and likely would remain that forever in the mind of the town—sat on a hill just on the edge of Antietam. Once it had been the property of a rich man who enjoyed its height, its expensive furnishings, its enviable view. It had stood there while the bloodiest day of the Civil War raged around it. It had stood while a wounded young soldier was murdered on its polished grand staircase. There it had remained while the mistress of the house grieved herself to death. Or so the legend went.

It had stood, falling into decay, disuse, disregard. Its stones had not moved when its porches rotted, when its windows were shattered by rocks heaved by rambunctious children. It had stood, empty but for its ghosts, for decades.

Until Rafe MacKade had returned and claimed it.

It was the house, Devin thought as he turned up its steep lane, that had brought Rafe and Regan together. Together, they had turned that brooding old building into something fine, something lovely.

Where there had once been weeds and thorny brambles, there was now a lush, terraced lawn, vivid with flowers and shrubs. He had helped plant them himself. The MacKades always united when it came to developing dreams—or destroying enemies.

The windows gleamed now, framed by rich blue trim, their overflowing flower boxes filled with sunny-faced pansies. The sturdy double porches were painted that same blue, and offered guests a place to sit and look toward town.

Or, he knew, if they chose to sit around at the back, they'd have a long view of the haunted woods that bordered the inn's property, his own farm, and the land where his brother Jared, his wife, Savannah, and their children lived.

He didn't knock, but simply stepped inside. There were no cars in the drive, but for Cassie's, so he knew the overnight guests had already left, and any others had yet to arrive.

He stood for a moment in the grand hall, with its polished floor, pretty rugs and haunted staircase. There were always flowers. Cassie saw to that. Pretty vases of fragrant blooms, little bowls and dishes with potpourri that he knew she made herself.

So, to him, the house always smelled like Cassie.

He wasn't sure where he would find her—in the kitchen, in the yard, in her apartment on the third floor. He moved through the house from front to rear, knowing that if he didn't find her in the first two, he would climb the outside stairs and knock on the door of her private quarters.

It was hard to believe that less than two years before, the house had been full of dust and cobwebs, all cracked plaster and chipped molding. Now floors and walls gleamed, windows shone, wood was polished to a high sheen. Antique tables were topped with what Devin always thought of as dust collectors, but they were charming.

Rafe and Regan had done something here, built something here. Just as they were doing in the old house they'd bought for themselves outside of town.

He envied his brother that, not just the love, but the partnership of a woman, the home and family they had created together.

Shane had the farm. Technically, it belonged to all four of them, but it was Shane's, heart and soul. Rafe had Regan and their baby, the inn, and the lovely old stone-and-cedar house they were making their own. Jared had Savannah, the children, and the cabin.

And as for himself? Devin mused. Well, he had the town, he supposed. And a cot in the back room of the sheriff's office.

The kitchen was empty. Though it was as neat as a model on display, it held all the warmth kitchens were meant to. Slate blue tiles and creamy white appliances were a backdrop for little things—fresh fruit in an old stoneware bowl, a sassy cookie jar in the shape of a smiling cat that he knew would be full of fresh, home-baked cookies, long, tapered jars that held the herbed vinegars Cassie made, a row of African violets in bloom on the wide windowsill over the sink.

And then, through the window, he saw her, taking billowing sheets from the line where they'd dried in the warm breeze.

His heart turned over in his chest. He could handle that, had handled it for too many years to count. She looked happy, was all he could think. Her lips were curved a little, her gray eyes dreamy. The breeze that fluttered the sheets teased her hair, sending the honeycomb curls dancing around her face, along her neck and throat.

Like the kitchen, she was neat, tidy, efficient without being cold. She wore a white cotton blouse tucked into navy slacks. Just lately, she'd started to add little pieces of jewelry. No rings. Her divorce had been final for a full year now, and he knew the exact day she'd taken off her wedding ring.

But she wore small gold hoops in her ears and a touch of color on her mouth. She'd stopped wearing makeup and jewelry shortly after her marriage. Devin remembered that, too.

Just as he remembered the first time he'd been called out to the house she rented with Joe, answering a complaint from the neighbors. He remembered the fear in her eyes when she'd come to the door, the marks on her face, the way her voice had hitched and trembled when she told him there wasn't any trouble, there was no trouble at all. She'd slipped and fallen, that was all.

Yes, he remembered that. And his frustration, the hideous sense of impotence that first time, and all the other times he'd had to confront her, to ask her, to quietly offer her alternatives that were just as quietly refused.

There'd been nothing he could do as sheriff to stop what happened inside that house, until the day she finally came into his office—bruised, beaten, terrified—to fill out a complaint.

There was little he could do now as sheriff but offer her friendship.

So he walked out the rear door, a casual smile on his face. "Hey, Cass."

Alarm came into her eyes first, darkening that lovely gray. He was used to it, though it pained him immeasurably to know that she thought of him as the sheriff first—as authority, as the bearer of trouble—before she thought of him as an old friend. But the smile came back more quickly than it once had, chasing the tension away from those delicate features.

"Hello, Devin." Calmly, because she was teaching herself to be calm, she hooked a clothespin back on the line and began folding the sheet.

"Need some help?"

Before she could refuse, he was plucking clothespins. She simply couldn't get used to a man doing such things. Especially such a man. He was so...big. Broad shoulders, big hands, long legs. And gorgeous, of course. All the MacKades were.

There was something so male about Devin, she couldn't really explain it. Even as he competently took linen from the line, folded it into the basket, he was all man. Unlike his deputies, he didn't wear the khaki uniform of his office, just jeans and a faded blue shirt rolled up to the elbows. There were muscles there, she'd seen them. And she had reason to be wary of a man's strength. But despite his big hands, his big shoulders, he'd never been anything but gentle. She tried to remember that as he brushed against her, reaching for another clothespin.

Still, she stepped away, kept distance between them. He smiled at her, and she tried to think of something to say. It would be easier if everything about him

wasn't so...definite, she supposed. So vivid. His hair
was as black as midnight, and curled over the frayed
collar of his shirt. His eyes were as green as moss.
Even the bones in his face were defined and impossible to ignore, the way they formed hollows and planes.
His mouth was firm, and that dimple beside it con-
stantly drew the eye.

He even smelled like a man. Plain soap, plain sweat.
He'd never been anything but kind to her, and he'd
been a part of her life forever, it seemed. But whenever it was just the two of them, she found herself as
nervous as a cat faced with a bulldog.

"Too nice a day to toss these in the dryer."

"What?" She blinked, then cursed herself. "Oh,
yes. I like hanging the linens out, when there's time.
We had two guests overnight, and we're expecting another couple later today. We're booked solid for the
Memorial Day weekend."

"You'll be busy."

"Yes. It's hardly like work, though, really."

He watched her smooth sheets into the basket. "Not
like waiting tables at Ed's."

"No." She smiled a little, then struggled with guilt.
"Ed was wonderful to me. She was great to work for."

"She's still ticked at Rafe for stealing you." Noting
the distress that leaped into her eyes, Devin shook his
head. "I'm only kidding, Cassie. You know she was
happy you took this job. How are the kids?"

"They're fine. Wonderful." Before she could pick
up the basket of linens herself, Devin had it tucked to
his hip, leaving her nothing to do with her hands.
"They'll be home soon, from school."

"No Little League practice today?"

"No." She headed toward the kitchen, but he opened the door before she could, and waited for her to go in ahead of him. "Connor's thrilled he made the team."

"He's the best pitcher they've got."

"Everyone says so." Automatically, she went to the stove to make coffee. "It's so strange. He was never interested in sports before...well, before," she finished lamely. "Bryan's been wonderful for him."

"My nephew's a hell of a kid."

There was such simple and honest pride in the statement that Cassie turned around to study him. "You think of him that way, really? I mean, even though there's no blood between you?"

"When Jared married Savannah, it made Bryan his son. That makes him my nephew. Family isn't just blood."

"No, and sometimes blood kin is more trouble than not."

"Your mother's hassling you again."

She only moved her shoulder and turned back to finish the coffee. "She's just set in her ways." Shifting, she reached into one of the glass-fronted cabinets for a cup and a small plate. When Devin's hand curled over her shoulder, she jerked and nearly dropped the stoneware to the tiles.

He started to step back, then changed his mind. Instead, he turned her around so that they were face-to-face, and kept both of his hands on her shoulders. "She's still giving you a hard time about Joe?"

She had to swallow, but couldn't quite get her throat muscles to work. His hands were firm, but they weren't hurting. There was annoyance in his eyes, but no meanness. She ordered herself to be calm, not to lower her gaze.

"She doesn't believe in divorce."

"Does she believe in wife-beating?"

Now she did wince, did lower her gaze. Devin cursed himself and lowered his hands to his sides. "I'm sorry."

"No, it's all right. I don't expect you to understand. I can't understand myself anymore." Relieved that he'd stepped back, she turned to the cookie jar and filled the plate with chocolate chip and oatmeal cookies she'd baked that morning. "It doesn't seem to matter that I'm happy, that the kids are happy. It doesn't matter that the law says what Joe did to me was wrong. That he attacked Regan. It only matters that I broke my vows and divorced him."

"Are you happy, Cassie?"

"I'd stopped believing I could be, or even that I should be." She set the plate on the table, went to pour him coffee. "Yes, I am happy."

"Are you going to make me drink this coffee by myself?"

She stared at him a minute. It was still such a novel concept, the idea that she could sit down in the middle of the day with a friend. Taking matters into his own hands, he got out a second cup.

"So tell me..." After pouring her coffee, he held out a chair for her. "How do the tourists feel about spending the night in a haunted house?"

"Some of them are disappointed when they don't see or hear anything." Cassie lifted her cup and tried not to feel guilty that she wasn't doing some chore. "Rafe was clever to publicize the inn as haunted."

"He's always been clever."

"Yes, he has. A few people are nervous when they come down for breakfast, but most of them are...well, excited, I guess. They'll have heard doors slamming or voices, or have heard her crying."

"Abigail Barlow. The tragic mistress of the house, the compassionate Southern belle married to the Yankee murderer."

"Yes. They'll hear her, or smell her roses, or just feel something. We've only had one couple leave in the middle of the night." For once, her smile was quick, and just a little wicked. "They were both terrified."

"But you're not. It doesn't bother you to have ghosts wandering?"

"No."

He cocked his head. "Have you heard her? Abigail?"

"Oh, yes, often. Not just at night. Sometimes when I'm alone here, making beds or tidying up, I'll hear her. Or feel her."

"And it doesn't spook you?"

"No, I feel..." She started to say "connected," but thought it would sound foolish. "Sorry for her. She was trapped and unhappy, married to a man who despised her, in love with someone else—"

"In love with someone else?" Devin asked, interrupting her. "I've never heard that."

Baffled, Cassie set her cup down with a little clink. "I haven't, either. I just—" *Know it,* she realized. "I suppose I added it in. It's more romantic. Emma calls her the lady. She likes to go into the bridal suite."

"And Connor?"

"It's a big adventure for him. All of it. They love it here. Once when Bryan was spending the night, I caught the three of them sneaking down to the guest floor. They wanted to go ghost-hunting."

"My brothers and I spent the night here when we were kids."

"Did you? Of course you did," she said before he could comment. "The MacKades and an empty, derelict, haunted house. They belong together. Did you go ghost-hunting?"

"I didn't have to. I saw her. I saw Abigail."

Cassie's smile faded. "You did?"

"I never told the guys. They'd have ragged on me for the rest of my life. But I saw her, sitting in the parlor, by the fire. There was a fire, I could smell it, feel the heat from the flames, smell the roses that were in a vase on the table beside her. She was beautiful," Devin said quietly. "Blond hair and porcelain skin, eyes the color of the smoke going up the flue. She wore a blue dress. I could hear the silk rustle as she moved. She was embroidering something, and her hands were small and delicate. She looked right at me, and she smiled. She smiled, but there were tears in her eyes. She spoke to me."

"She spoke to you," Cassie repeated, as chills raced up and down her back like icy fingers. "What did she say?"

"'If only.'" Devin brought himself back, shook himself. "That was it. 'If only.' Then she was gone, and I told myself I'd been dreaming. But I knew I hadn't. I always hoped I'd see her again."

"But you haven't?"

"No, but I've heard her weeping. It breaks my heart."

"I know."

"I'd, ah, appreciate it if you wouldn't mention that to Rafe. He'd still rag on me."

"I won't." She smiled as he bit into a cookie. "Is that why you come here, hoping to see her again?"

"I come to see you." The minute he'd said it, he recognized his mistake. Her face went from relaxed to wary in the blink of an eye. "And the kids," he added quickly. "And for the cookies."

She relaxed again. "I'll put some in a bag for you to take with you." But even as she rose to do so, he covered her hand with his. She froze, not in fear so much as from the shock of the contact. Speechless, she stared down at the way his hand swallowed hers.

"Cassie . . ." He strained against the urge to gather her up, just to hold her, to stroke those flyaway curls, to taste, finally to taste, that small, serious mouth.

There was a hitch in her breathing that she was afraid to analyze. But she made herself shift her gaze, ordered herself not to be so much a coward that she couldn't look into his eyes. She wished she knew what she was looking at, or looking for. All she knew was that it was more than the patience and pity she'd expected to see there, that it was different.

"Devin—" She broke off, jerked back at the sound of giggles and stomping feet. "The kids are home," she finished quickly, breathlessly, and hurried to the door. "I'm down here!" she called out, knowing that they would do as they'd been told and go directly to the apartment unless she stopped them.

"Mama, I got a gold star on my homework." Emma came in, a blond pixie in a red playsuit. She set her lunch box on the counter and smiled shyly at Devin. "Hello."

"There's my best girl. Let's see that star."

Clutching the lined paper in her hand, she walked to him. "You have a star."

"Not as pretty as this one." Devin traced a finger over the gold foil stuck to the top of the paper. "Did you do this by yourself?"

"Almost all. Can I sit in your lap?"

"You bet." He plucked her up, cradled her there. He quite simply adored her. After brushing his cheek against her hair, he grinned over at Connor. "How's it going, champ?"

"Okay." A little thrill moved through Connor at the nickname. He was small for his age, like Emma, and blond, though at ten he had hair that was shades darker than his tow-headed sister's.

"You pitched a good game last Saturday."

Now he flushed. "Thanks. But Bryan went four for five." His loyalty and love for his best friend knew no bounds. "Did you see?"

"I was there for a few innings. Watched you smoke a few batters."

"Connor got an A on his history test," Emma said. "And that mean old Bobby Lewis shoved him and called him a bad name when we were in line for the bus."

"Emma..." Mortified, Connor scowled at his sister.

"I guess Bobby Lewis didn't get an A," Devin commented.

"Bryan fixed him good," Emma went on.

I bet he did, Devin thought, and handed Emma a cookie so that she'd be distracted enough to stop embarrassing her brother.

"I'm proud of you." Trying not to worry, Cassie gave Connor a quick squeeze. "Both of you. A gold star and an A all in one day. We'll have to celebrate later with ice-cream sundaes from Ed's."

"It's no big deal," Connor began.

"It is to me." Cassie bent down and kissed him firmly. "A very big deal."

"I used to struggle with math," Devin said casually. "Never could get more than a C no matter what I did."

Connor stared at the floor, weighed down by the stigma of being bright. He could still hear his father berating him. *Egghead. Pansy. Useless.*

Cassie started to speak, to defend, but Devin sent her one swift look.

"But then, I used to ace history and English."

Stunned, Connor jerked his head up and stared. "You did?"

It was a struggle, but Devin kept his eyes sober. The kid didn't mean to be funny, or insulting, he knew.

"Yeah. I guess it was because I liked to read a lot. Still do."

"You read books?" It was an epiphany for Connor. Here was a man who held a real man's job and who liked to read.

"Sure." Devin jiggled Emma on his knee and smiled. "The thing was, Rafe was pitiful in English, but he was a whiz in math. So we traded off. I'd do his—" He glanced at Cassie, realized his mistake. "I'd help him with his English homework and he'd help me with the math. It got us both through."

"Do you like to read stories?" Connor wanted to know. "Made-up stories?"

"They're the best kind."

"Connor writes stories," Cassie said, even as Connor wriggled in embarrassment.

"So I've heard. Maybe you'll let me read one." Before the boy could answer, Devin's beeper went off. "Hell," he muttered.

"Hell," Emma said adoringly.

"You want to get me in trouble?" he asked, then hitched her onto his hip as he rose to call in. A few minutes later, he'd given up on his idea of wheedling his way into a dinner invitation. "Gotta go. Somebody broke into the storeroom at Duff's and helped themselves to a few cases of beer."

"Will you shoot them?" Emma asked him.

"I don't think so. How about a kiss?"

She puckered up obligingly before he set her down. "Thanks for the coffee, Cass."

"I'll walk you out. You two go on upstairs and get your after-school snack," she told her children. "I'll be right along." She waited until they were nearly at the front door before she spoke again. "Thank you for talking to Connor like that. He's still so sensitive about liking school."

"He's a bright kid. It won't take much longer for him to start appreciating himself."

"You helped. He admires you."

"It didn't take any effort to tell him I like to read." Devin paused at the door. "He means a lot to me. All of you do." When she opened her mouth to speak, he took a chance and brushed a finger over her cheek. "All of you do," he repeated, and walked out, leaving her staring after him.

Chapter 2

Some nights, late at night, when her children were sleeping and the guests were settled down, Cassie would roam the house. She was careful not to go on the second floor, where guests were bedded down in the lovely rooms and suites Rafe and Regan had built.

They paid for privacy, and Cassie was careful to give it.

But she was free to walk through her own apartment on the third floor, to admire the rooms, the view from the windows, even the feel of the polished hardwood under her bare feet.

It was a freedom, and a security, that she knew she would never take for granted. Any more than she would take for granted the curtains framing the windows, made of fabric that she had chosen and paid for herself. Or the kitchen table, the sofa, each lamp.

Not all new, she mused, but new to her. Everything that had been in the house she shared with Joe had been sold. It had been her way of sweeping away the past. Nothing here was from her before. It had been vital to her to start this life with nothing she hadn't brought into it on her own.

If she was restless, she could go down on the main level, move from parlor to sitting room, into the beautiful solarium, with its lovely plants and glistening glass. She could stand in the hallways, sit on the steps. Simply enjoy the quiet and solitude.

The only room she avoided was the library. It was the only room that never welcomed her, despite its deep leather chairs and walls of books.

She knew instinctively that it had been Charles Barlow's realm. Abigail's husband. The master of the house. A man who had shot, in cold blood, a wounded Confederate soldier hardly old enough to shave.

Sometimes she felt the horror and sadness of that when she walked up and down the staircase where it had happened. Now and again she even heard the shot, the explosion of it, and the screams of the servants who had witnessed the senseless and brutal murder.

But she understood senseless brutality, knew it existed.

Just as she knew Abigail still existed, in this house. It wasn't just the sound of weeping, the scent of roses that would come suddenly and from nowhere. It was just the feel of the air, that connection that she'd been too embarrassed to mention to Devin.

That was how she knew Abigail had loved a man who wasn't her husband. That she had longed for him, wept for him, as well as for the murdered boy. That she had dreamed of him, and despaired of ever knowing the joy of real love.

Cassie understood, and sympathized. That was why she felt so welcomed in this house that held so much of the past. Why she was never afraid.

No, she was grateful for every hour she spent here as caretaker to beautiful things. It had been nearly a year since she had accepted Regan's and Rafe's offer and moved her family in. She was still dazzled that they would trust her with the job, and she worked hard to earn that trust.

The work was all pleasure, she thought now, as she wandered into the parlor. To tend and polish lovely antiques, to cook breakfast in that wonderful kitchen and serve it to guests on pretty dishes. To have flowers all around the house, inside and out.

It was like a dream, like one of the fairy tales Savannah MacKade illustrated.

She was so rarely afraid anymore, hardly even disturbed by the nightmares that had plagued her for so long she'd come to expect them. It was unusual for her to wake shivering in the middle of the night, out of a dream—listening, terrified, for Joe's steps, for his voice.

She was safe here, and, for the first time in her life, free.

Bundled into her robe, she curled on the window seat in the parlor. She wouldn't stay long. Her children slept deeply and were content here, but there was always a chance they might wake and need her. But she wanted just a few moments alone to hug her good fortune close to her heart.

She had a home where her children could laugh and play and feel safe. It was wonderful to see how quickly Emma was throwing off her shyness and becoming a bright, chattering little girl. Childhood had been harder on Connor, she knew. It shamed her to realize that he had seen and heard so much more of the misery than she had guessed. But he was coming out of his shell.

It relieved her to see how comfortable they were with Devin, with all the MacKades, really. There had been a time when Emma hesitated to so much as speak to a man, and Connor, sweet, sensitive Connor had forever been braced for a verbal blow.

No more.

Just that day, both of them had talked to Devin as if it were as natural as breathing. She wished she was as resilient. It was the badge, she decided. She was finding it easier and easier to be comfortable with Jared or Rafe or Shane. She didn't jolt when one of them touched her or flashed that MacKade grin.

It was different with Devin. But then, she'd had to go to him, had to confess that she'd allowed herself to be beaten and abused for years, had been forced to show him the marks on her body. Nothing, not even Joe's vicious fists, had ever humiliated her more than that.

She knew he was sorry for her, and felt obligated to look out for her and the children. He took his responsibilities as sheriff seriously. No one, including her-

self, would have believed twelve or fifteen years
before, when he and his brothers were simply those
bad MacKade boys, that they would turn out the way
they had.

Devin had made himself into an admirable man.
Still rough, she supposed. She knew he could break up
a bar fight with little more than a snarl, and that he
used his fists when that didn't work.

Still, she'd never known anyone gentler or more
compassionate. He'd been very good to her and her
children, and she owed him.

Laying her cheek against the window, she closed her
eyes. She was going to train herself not to be so jumpy
around him. She could do it. She had been working
very hard over the past year or so to teach herself
composure and calm, to pretend she wasn't shy when
she greeted the guests. It worked so well that she often didn't even feel shy anymore.

There were even times, and they were coming more
and more often, when she actually felt competent.

So she would work now to teach herself not to be so
jittery around Devin. She would stop thinking about
his badge and remember that he was one of her oldest
friends—one she'd even had a little crush on, once
upon a time. She would stop thinking of how big his
hands were, or what would happen if he got angry and
used them against her.

Instead she would remember how gently they ruffled her daughter's hair, or how firmly they covered
her son's when he helped him with his batting stance.

Or how nice it had been, how unexpectedly nice, to
feel the way his finger brushed her cheek.

She curled more comfortably on the padded seat....

He was here, right here beside her, smiling in that way that brought his dimple out and made odd things happen to her insides. He touched her, and she didn't jolt this time. There, she thought, it was working already.

He was touching her, drawing her against him. Oh, his body was hard. But she didn't flinch. She was trembling, though. Couldn't stop. He was so big, so strong, he could break her in half. And yet... and yet his hands stroked so lightly over her. Over her skin. But he couldn't be touching her there.

His mouth was on hers, so warm and gentle. She couldn't stop him. She forgot that she should, even when his tongue slid over hers and his hand cupped her breast as if it were the most natural thing in the world.

He was touching her, and it was hard to breathe, because those big hands were gliding over her. And now his mouth. Oh, it was wrong, it had to be wrong, but it was so wonderful to feel that warm, wet mouth on her.

She was whimpering, moaning, opening for him. She felt him coming inside her, so hard, so smooth, so right.

The explosion of a gunshot had her jerking upright. She was gasping for breath, damp with sweat, her mind a muddled mess.

Alone in the parlor. Of course she was alone. But her skin was tingling, and there was a tingling, almost a burning inside her, that she hadn't felt in so many years she'd forgotten it was possible.

Shame washed over her, had her gathering her robe tight at her throat. It was terrible, she thought, just terrible, to have been imagining herself with Devin like that. After he'd been so kind to her.

She didn't know what had gotten into her. She didn't even like sex. It was something she'd learned to dread, and then to tolerate, very soon after her miserable wedding-night initiation. Pleasure had never entered into it. She simply wasn't built for that kind of pleasure, and had accepted the lack early on.

But when she got to her feet, her legs were shaky and there was a nagging pressure low in her stomach. She drew in a breath, and along with it the delicate scent of roses.

So she wasn't alone, Cassie thought. Abigail was with her. Comforted, she went back upstairs to check on her children one last time before going to bed.

Devin was well into what he considered the paper-pushing part of the day by noon. He had a report to type and file on the break-in at Duff's Tavern. The trio of teenagers who'd thought to relieve Duff of a bit of his inventory had been pathetically easy to track down.

Then there was the traffic accident out on Brook Lane. Hardly more than a fender bender, Devin mused as he hammered at the keys, but Lester Swoop, whose new sedan had been crinkled, was raising a ruckus.

He had to finish up his report to the mayor and town council on the preparations for crowd control on parade day.

Then, maybe, he'd get some lunch.

Across the office, his young deputy, Donnie Banks, was dealing with parking tickets. And, as usual, drumming his fingers on the metal desk to some inner rhythm that Devin tried hard to ignore.

The day was warm enough that the windows were open. The budget didn't run to air-conditioning. He could hear the sounds of traffic—what there was of it—and the occasionally squeal of brakes as someone came up too fast on the stop light at Main and Antietam.

He still had the mail to sort through, his job, since Crystal Abbott was off on maternity leave and he hadn't come up with a temporary replacement for her position as general dogsbody.

He didn't mind really. The sheer monotony of paperwork could be soothing. Things were quiet, as they were expected to be in a town of less than twenty-five hundred. His job was to keep it that way, and deal with the drunk-and-disorderlies, the traffic violations, the occasional petty theft or domestic dispute.

Things heated up now and again, but in his seven years with Antietam's sheriff's department, both as deputy and as sheriff, he'd had to draw his weapon only twice. And he'd never been forced to fire it.

Reason and guile usually worked, and if they didn't, a fist usually turned the tide.

When the phone rang, Devin glanced hopefully toward his deputy. Donnie's fingers never broke rhythm, so, with a sigh, Devin answered the phone himself. He was well on his way to calming a hysterical woman who claimed that her neighbor deliberately sent her dog over into her yard to fertilize her petunias when Jared walked in.

"Yes, ma'am. No, ma'am." Devin rolled his eyes and motioned Jared to a seat. "Have you talked with her, asked her to keep her dog in her own yard?"

The answer came so fast and loud that Devin winced and held the phone six inches from his ear. In the little wooden chair across the desk, Jared grinned and stretched out his legs.

"Yes, ma'am, I'm sure you worked very hard on your petunias. No, no, don't do that. Please. There's a law against discharging a firearm within town limits. You don't want to go waving your shotgun at the dog. I'm going to send somebody over there. Yes, ma'am, I surely am. Ah . . . we'll see what we can do. You leave that shotgun alone now, you hear? Yes, ma'am, I've got it all down right here. You just sit tight."

He hung up, tore off the memo sheet. "Donnie?"

"Yo."

"Get on over to Oak Leaf and handle this."

"We got us a situation?" Donnie stopped his drumming, looking hopeful. Devin thought he seemed very young, in his carefully pressed uniform, with his scarecrow hair and eager blue eyes.

"We've got a French poodle using a petunia bed as a toilet. Explain about the leash law, and see if you can keep these two women from a hair-pulling contest."

"Yo!" Delighted with the assignment, Donnie took the information sheet, adjusted his hat and strode out, ready to uphold the law.

"I think he started to shave last week," Devin commented.

"Petunias and poodles," Jared said, and stretched. "I can see you're busy."

"Antietam's a real naked city." Devin got up to pour them both coffee. "Had us a *situation* down to Duff's," he added, tinting his voice with Donnie's accent and emphasis. "Three cases of beer went missing."

"Well, well . . ."

"Got two of them back." After handing Jared the mug, Devin eased a hip onto his desk. "The other had been consumed by three sixteen-year-olds."

"Tracked them down, did you?"

"It didn't take Sam Spade." Devin shook his head as he sipped. "They'd bragged about it right and left, took the beer out to the field near the high school and had themselves a party. They were sick as dogs when I caught up with them. Idiots. Now they've got B and E charges, larceny, and an appointment with juvie."

"Seems to me I remember a couple of cases of beer and a party. In the woods."

"We didn't steal it," Devin reminded him. "We left Duff the money in the storeroom—after we'd broken in and taken the beer."

"A fine but salient point. God, we got drunk."

"And sick," Devin added. "When we crawled home, Mom made us shovel manure all afternoon. I thought I'd die."

"Those were the days," Jared said with a sigh. He sat back. Despite the trim suit and tie, the expensive shoes, there was no mistaking him for anything but a

MacKade. Like his brother, he had the reckless dark good looks. A bit more groomed, a bit more polished, but reckless enough.

"What are you doing in town?"

"This and that." Jared wanted to work up to what he had to tell Devin. "Layla's getting a tooth."

"Yeah? Keeping you guys up?"

"I forgot what sleep's like." His grin flashed. "It's great. You know, Bryan changes diapers. The kid's so in love with her, Savannah says the first thing he does when he gets home from school is to go find her."

"You got lucky," Devin murmured.

"Don't I know it. You ought to try it, Dev. Marriage is a pretty good deal."

"It's working for you and Rafe. I saw him this morning, heading into the hardware with Nate strapped to his back. He looked real domestic."

"Did you tell him that?"

"I didn't want to start a fight in front of the baby."

"Good call. You know what you need around here, Dev?" Still sipping coffee, Jared looked around the office. It was utilitarian, basic. Desks, wood floors, coffeepot, a ceiling fan that he knew squeaked when it was put into use in the summer, unpadded chairs, metal file cabinets. "You need a dog. Ethel'll be dropping that litter any day now."

Devin raised a brow. Fred and Ethel, Shane's golden retrievers had finally figured out what boy and girl dogs could do together besides chase rabbits. "Yeah, I need a puppy puddling on the floor and chewing up my papers."

"Companionship," Jared insisted. "Think how you'd look cruising around town with a dog riding shotgun. You could deputize him."

The image made Devin grin, but he set his coffee down. "I'll keep it in mind. Now why don't you tell me what you came in to tell me."

Jared blew out a breath. He knew how Devin's mind worked, step by meticulous step. He'd let Jared ramble, but he hadn't been fooled. "I had some business at the prison this morning."

"One of your clients not getting his full television rights?"

Jared set his coffee aside, linked his fingers. "You arrest them, I represent them. That's why it's called law and order."

"Right. How could I forget. So?"

"So. I had a meeting with the warden, and as he's aware that I'm Cassie's lawyer, he felt it reasonable to pass some news on to me."

Devin's mouth thinned. "Dolin."

"Yeah, Joe Dolin."

"He's not up for a parole hearing for another eighteen months." Devin knew the exact day, to the hour.

"That's right. It seems that after a difficult period of adjustment, during which Joe was a disciplinary problem, he's become a model prisoner."

"I'll bet."

Jared recognized the bitterness in the tone, understood it perfectly. "We know he's a bastard, Devin, but the point here is, he's playing the game. And he's playing it well."

"He won't make parole, not the first time at bat. I'll make sure of it."

"Parole's not the issue. Yet. He's been put on work release."

"The hell he has!"

"As of this week. I argued against it. I pointed out the fact that he'll be only a matter of miles from Cassie, his history of violence, his ties to the town." Feeling helpless, Jared unlinked his hands, held them palms up. "I got shot down. He'll be supervised, along with the rest of the crew. We need the work release program, need the park and the roads cleaned and maintained, and this is a cheap way to handle it. Letting cooperative prisoners serve the community is a solid method of rehabilitation."

"And when they take a hike from trash detail?" Devin was pacing now, eyes fiery. "It happens. Two or three times a year, at least, it happens. I hauled one back myself last fall."

"It happens," Jared agreed. "They rarely get far. They're pretty easy to spot in the prison uniform, and most of them don't know the area."

"Dolin knows the damn area."

"You're not going to get any arguments from me. I'm going to fight it, Devin. But it's not going to be easy. Not when Cassie's own mother has been writing the warden in Joe's defense."

"That bitch." Devin's hands curled into fists. "She knows what he did to Cassie. Cassie," he repeated, and scrubbed his hands over his face. "She's just starting to pull things together. What the hell is this going to do to her?"

"I'm heading over there now to tell her."

"No." Devin dropped his hands. "I'll tell her. You go file papers, or whatever you have to do to turn this thing around. I want that son of a bitch locked up, twenty-four hours a day."

"They've got a crew out on 34 right now. Trash detail. He's on it."

"Fine." Devin headed for the door. "That's just fine."

It didn't take him long to get there, or to spot the bright orange vests of the road crew. Devin pulled to the shoulder behind a pickup truck where bags of trash were already heaped.

He got out of his car, leaned against the hood and watched Joe Dolin.

The sixteen months in prison hadn't taken off any of his bulk, Devin noted. He was a big man, thick, burly. He'd been going to fat before his arrest. From the look of him, he'd been busy turning that fat into muscle.

The prison system approved of physical fitness.

He and another man were unclogging the runoff on the other side of the road, working systematically and in silence as they gathered up dead leaves, litter.

Devin bided his time, waited until Joe straightened, hauled a plastic bag over his shoulder and turned.

Their eyes met, held. Devin wondered what the warden would say about rehabilitation if he'd seen that look in Joe's eyes. The heat and the hate. If he'd seen that slow, bitterly triumphant smile before Joe tossed the bag in the bed of the pickup parked on his side of the road.

Because he knew himself, Devin stayed where he was. He knew that if he got close, too close, he wouldn't be able to stop himself. The badge he wore was both a responsibility and a barrier.

If he was a civilian, he could walk across the road, ram his fists into Joe's leering face and take the consequences. If he was a civilian, he could pummel the wife-beating bastard into putty.

But he wasn't a civilian.

"Help you, Sheriff?" One of the supervisors walked over, ready to chat, officer to officer. His easy smile faded at the look in Devin's eyes. "Is there a problem?"

"Depends." Devin took out one of the cigarettes he'd been working on giving up for the past two months. Taking his time, he struck a match, lit it, blew out smoke. "You see that man there, the big one?"

"Dolin? Sure."

"You remember that name." Devin flicked his gaze down to the ID clipped to the supervisor's shirt. "And I'm going to remember yours, Richardson. If he gets away from you, even for a heartbeat, it's going to be your ass."

"Hey, look, Sheriff—"

Devin merely fixed his eyes on Richardson's face, kept them there as he pushed off the hood. "You make sure that son of a bitch doesn't wander into my town, Richardson. You make damn sure of it."

Joe watched the sheriff's car pull out, drive away. He bent his back to the work, like a good team player.

And patted his pocket, where the latest letter from his mother-in-law was tucked.

He knew what it said, almost word for word. She kept him up with Cassie just fine. How the little bitch had a fancy job now at the MacKade Inn. Lousy MacKades. He was going to take care of all of them, every last one of them, when he got out.

But first he was going to take care of Cassie.

She thought she could have him tossed in a cell. She thought she could divorce him and start strutting her stuff around town. Well, she was going to think again, real soon.

Her mama was helping him out, writing him letters. They were preachy letters, and he couldn't stand the dried up old bat, but she was helping him out. And he wrote her every week, telling her how he'd suffered, how he'd gotten religion, how he wanted to be with his family again. He made sure he went on about the kids.

He could have cared less about the kids. Whiny little brats.

It was Cassie he wanted. She was his wife—till death do us part. He was going to be reminding her of that before too much longer.

He hauled another bag to the bed of the truck, tossed it in. Oh, yeah, he was going to remind her good, just like the old days. She would pay, in spades, for every hour he'd spent in a cell.

Curling his hand into a fist, he dreamed about his homecoming.

Chapter 3

Instead of going directly to Cassie, Devin went to the prison. He didn't doubt Jared's skill as a lawyer, but he wanted, needed, to add his weight. He forced himself to stay calm as he laid out the facts, and his opinion, to the warden.

For every protest he made, he was shown a report to offset it. Joe Dolin had indeed made himself into a model prisoner, one who showed every sign of rehabilitation. He worked hard, followed the rules, went to chapel regularly. He expressed regret over his crimes and kept up with his alcohol-abuse counseling.

When Devin left, he understood that the system he worked hard to uphold had just kicked him in the teeth. All he could do now was tell Cassie and try to reassure her.

He found her on her hands and knees in the parlor, polishing the carved wood of a gateleg table. She was so busy humming to herself, she hadn't heard him come in. She was wearing a white bib apron over her blouse and slacks, and had a plastic basket beside her filled with rags and cleaning tools.

Her wavy hair was tucked behind her ear to keep it from falling forward into her face. She'd been letting it grow some, he thought. It rippled just past her chin.

She looked so damn happy, Devin thought, and jammed his hands into his pockets.

"Cass?"

She jerked up, barely missed rapping her head on the table extension. Then blushed right to the hairline.

"Devin." She twisted her polishing rag in her hands as her nerves went into overdrive. She'd been replaying the dream in her head, the dream she'd had right here in the parlor, on the window seat. The dream where Devin had ... Oh, my ...

He stared at her, then stepped forward. She looked as though she'd been caught rifling the till. "What's wrong? What's the matter?"

"Nothing. Nothing." It seemed her stomach was suddenly full of bats and she had to hold back a nervous giggle. "My mind was wandering, that's all." Was it ever. "And you startled me. That's all."

It wasn't like her to keep repeating herself, and his gaze narrowed. "Are you sure you're all right?"

"Yes, yes. Fine. Just fine." She scrambled to her feet, still twisting the rag. "The couple who are staying here went out to tour the battlefield. They're going to stay another night. They're from North Carolina. He's a battlefield junkie. That's what he said. I gave them all the pamphlets, and . . . and a tour of the house. They wanted to see all of it. They're excited about the idea of ghosts.''

Puzzled, he nodded. She was babbling like a brook, when he usually had to coax to get three sentences in a row out of her. "Okay."

"Do you want some coffee? I'll get you some coffee," she said, and started to bolt before he could answer. "And brownies. I made brownies this morning, and—" When he put a hand on her arm to stop her, she froze like a doe caught in headlights.

"Cassandra, relax."

"I am relaxed. I'm relaxed." His hand was firm, warm. She thought she could feel the texture of it through her skin, all the way to the bone.

"You're about to jump out of your shoes. Take a deep breath. Take a couple of them."

Obediently she did, and felt some of the nerves settle. "I'm fine, Devin."

"Okay, we'll have some coffee." But even as he started to lead her out, his beeper went off. "Damn it." He strode to the candlestick phone on the gateleg to call in. "MacKade. Yes, Donnie."

Devin pressed his fingers against his eyes. Where had the headache come from, and why the hell was Cassie staring at him as if he'd grown two pounding heads?

"I'm on a call now, Donnie. Handle it. That's what I said. Look, put the damn poodle in lockup, along with those idiot women, if you have to, but—" He broke off, cursed himself, knowing Donnie would do exactly that.

"Abort that. Be diplomatic, Donnie, and do your job. You're going to have to fine the poodle lady, but do it privately and professionally. Suggest a fence. Remind her that the leash law is there for her pup's safety, as well as the public's. There's traffic on that street, and her little dog could get himself squashed. When you've handled that, you go over to the complainant, tell her it's been dealt with, and compliment her on her flowers. Suggest a fence. You know, how good fences make good neighbors. No, I didn't make that up. Go away, Donnie."

He hung up and turned to see Cassie smiling at him. "A small dog problem," he explained.

"You're so good at that, and knowing how to handle people and put things right."

"I'm a regular Solomon." He blew out a breath. "Sit down, Cassie. I need to talk to you."

"Oh." Her smile faded. "Something's wrong."

"Not necessarily. Come on, let's sit down." Because he wanted to be able to hold her hand when he told her, he chose the curvy settee that always made him feel like a clumsy giant. "I'm going to tell you first that there's nothing to worry about. That I don't want you to worry."

"It's about Joe." Her hand trembled once in his, then went still. "They let him out."

"No." He squeezed her hand gently, reassuringly, and kept his eyes steady on hers. "He's not going to be out of jail for a long time."

"He wants to see the children." She went dead pale, her eyes huge and dark and terrified. "Oh, God, Devin, the children."

"No." He cursed himself, knowing he was only making it worse by trying to cushion the blow. "It's nothing like that. It's the work release program. You know what that is."

"Yes, they let the prisoners out for a few hours to do jobs, community service. Oh." A single shudder escaped before she closed her eyes. "That's it."

"He's working on a road crew. Trash and litter pickup. That sort of thing. I wanted you to know, and not worry. I've arranged to be informed of his schedule. I'll know exactly where he is, and so will you. I don't want you driving by one day and seeing him on the side of the road and getting scared."

"All right." The fear was there, but she could handle it. She'd handled worse. "He's supervised."

"That's right." He wasn't going to bring up how often they misplaced a prisoner. She'd know it already. "I'm going to drive by, or have one of the men drive by, wherever he's working, a couple of times a day. And, because I want you to feel secure about this, we'll do drive-bys here, too."

And at the school, he thought, but he didn't want to bring up the kids again.

"He's still in prison," she said, to reassure herself. "There are guards."

"That's right. Jared's working on a protest, but I should tell you— Damn it." He let out another breath. "Your mother's for it, and she's been writing to the warden."

"I knew that." Cassie squared her shoulders. "She and Joe are writing each other. She's showed me his letters. It doesn't make any difference, Devin. I'm never going back to that. I'm never letting my children go back to that. We'll be all right."

"You'll be fine." He was going to see to it. He tucked a stray curl behind her ear, relieved that she didn't jolt. "I'm sorry I scared you."

"You didn't. Not really."

"Anytime, Cassie, day or night, that you feel uncomfortable or uneasy, I want you to call me. You know I spend most nights at the office. I can be here in five minutes if you need me."

"I never feel uncomfortable or uneasy here. I'm hardly ever alone." When he lifted a brow, she smiled. "Can't you smell them?"

"The roses? Yeah." Now he smiled. "Still, I'm usually better company than a ghost. You call me."

"All right." She had to draw together all her courage. A point had to be proved. He was her friend, always had been. She had to stop being a trembling little mouse. "Thank you." She made herself smile, then laid a hand on his cheek, and touched her lips to his.

He barely tasted her, but the explosion ripped through his system like napalm. It was so unexpected, so long desired. He didn't realize his hand had tightened like a vise on her fingers, making her eyes go wide with shock. All he knew was that her lips had been on his, just for an instant.

And he couldn't stand it.

He dragged her against him, and captured that taste again, devoured it, steeped himself in it. Warm, sweet.

The shape of her mouth, that deep dip, drove him crazy. He crushed it under his, traced it with a frantic tongue, then dived deep to plunder.

His heart was thundering, wild surf against jagged rocks. His blood was racing, making his head buzz. She was everything soft and small and sweet, everything he craved, everything he cherished.

It took him several desperate moments to realize her hands were trapped between them. And she was rigid in his arms. Stunned, he let her go and leaped up in one frenzied motion.

And she stared at him, eyes dark as rain clouds, one hand lifted to lie against the mouth he'd just savaged.

That was the word for it, he thought, disgusted. Savaged.

"I'm sorry." He was as pale now as she was flushed, and cursing himself viciously. "I'm sorry," he said again. "I'm . . . sorry. I didn't mean to— You caught me off guard." There was no excuse, he reminded himself, and his punishment for breaking her trust would be the losing of it. "That was way out of line, and it won't happen again. I don't know what I was thinking of. I have to go."

"Devin—"

"I have to go," he repeated, almost desperately, as he backed up. He nearly tripped over a table, decided that would have capped things off nicely. Because she hadn't moved an inch, he was able to escape without further humiliating himself.

She listened to the door slamming behind him. No, she hadn't moved, because she couldn't. She didn't think it would be wise to try to stand just yet.

What had just happened here? she asked herself. She had kissed him, thinking it was time she was able to make that friendly gesture.

Rafe kissed her all the time. When he came by the inn for something, he often kissed her, just the way she'd tried to kiss Devin. Lightly, casually. And after a while, she'd gotten used to it, and she no longer stiffened up.

Then Devin had kissed her. But he didn't kiss like Rafe at all. No, not at all. She still had her fingers against her lips, and could still feel the heat there. No, she'd never been kissed like that before, by anyone. As if the man's life had depended on it. She'd never imagined Devin...

Oh, but she had, she remembered, letting her unsteady hand fall into her lap. She had imagined, just the night before. Had she dreamed her way into this?

What had happened here was certainly reality. Her heart was pounding still, and her skin was hot. She'd been so shocked by what he'd done, the way he'd grabbed her, the way his mouth had covered hers, she hadn't been able to move.

How long had it lasted? Thirty seconds, a minute? She couldn't say, but so much had happened inside her. She was still shaky from it.

He'd been sorry. Of course he had, she thought, and leaned back, closed her eyes and tried to catch her breath. He hadn't meant to kiss her. It had just been some sort of spontaneous reaction. A male reaction. Then he'd found her lacking and let her go. Apologized. He was a good and honorable man, and he'd apologized for doing something he hadn't really meant to do.

It was just a kiss, she reminded herself, but had to press a hand to her jittery stomach. Now she'd spoiled things, because she hadn't been able to shrug it off, or laugh it off like a normal woman. Any more than she'd been able to respond to him and make him want to kiss her again.

She would make an effort, Cassie ordered herself, to behave as though nothing had happened. The very next time she saw him, she would smile and make natural conversation. She was getting better at those things. She simply couldn't bear it if they couldn't be friends anymore.

She got up on still-wobbly legs to finish her polishing. And didn't think of Joe Dolin at all.

Devin worked like a fiend the rest of the day and all of the next. He drove his deputies insane, and drove out to the farm to extend the same courtesy to his younger brother.

Of course, he told himself he'd come out to work. There were crops to be tended, and several of the cows that hadn't yet calved were due to drop. He found his services welcomed when one of the cows delivered breech.

By the time it was over and the new calf was teetering on its spindly legs, Devin was a mess. His shirt was ruined, his arm was bruised from being contracted inside the cow's birth canal. And he stank.

In the stall, Shane was equally dirty, and he was whistling cheerfully as he administered inoculations to the annoyed baby. "There you go, pal. That didn't hurt much."

Disgusted, Devin stared at him. It had been a hard, messy job, and it wasn't over. The stall would have to be cleaned out and fresh hay spread, and the calf would need watching for the next couple of hours.

And there was Shane, kneeling in the muck, happy as a fool.

He'd been letting his hair grow lately, Devin noted, and he'd pulled a tail of it through the opening in the back of his grimy cap. His green eyes, shades paler than Devin's, were dreamy, and his mouth was curved next to his dimple. He was sinfully good-looking, even for a MacKade. And he was the baby of the family, even younger than Devin, which meant that his older brothers had been honor-bound to kick his butt well and often.

As he continued to whistle, Devin gave serious thought to doing so now. "What the hell are you so happy about?"

"Nice healthy calf, from the look of him." Despite the calf's strong objections, Shane was holding him still and examining his eyes and ears. "Mama's doing fine now. What's not to be happy about?"

"She damn near broke my arm."

"She couldn't help it," Shane said reasonably. "Besides, I told you I'd take that end. You insisted."

"Yeah, right. This place is a mess."

"Birthing's not neat." Shane stood and rubbed his filthy hands on his equally filthy jeans. He stepped out of the stall and leaned against the open door. "Besides, I thought this might sweat the mood out of you." His grin was cocky, confident—all the more reason for Devin to want to punch it in. "Women trouble, right?"

"I don't have women trouble."

"That's 'cause you don't have any women—which, I might add, is an embarrassment to all of us. Why don't you take one of mine? I've got plenty."

Devin answered the suggestion with the crude and expected response before he stepped over to the sink to wash his hands.

"No, really. You know who I think would be good for you? Frannie Spader. She's got all this red hair that just sort of tumbles all over the place, and the cutest smile. And when you get past the hair and the smile, she's got a body that can make a man whimper. I don't think you've done nearly enough whimpering lately."

"I'll pick my own women. I don't need your damn cast-offs."

"Just being brotherly." He slapped Devin on the back before reaching for the soap. "Of course, if you weren't so damn brotherly yourself, you could probably be making time with little Cassie—"

It was a tribute to Devin's speed, and Shane's innocence, that the blow caught Shane solidly on the jaw and sent him flying. He landed hard, shook his head. Before he could ask Devin what the devil had gotten into him, he was assaulted by a hundred and seventy-five pounds of furious, frustrated male.

They were well matched, knew each other's moves and rhythms. The barn echoed with grunts, the smack of flesh against bone, curses, as they rolled over the dusty concrete floor.

"Oh, for heaven's sake."

The female voice, and the disdain in it, didn't register on either of the combatants. Shane dropped his guard just long enough to be rewarded with a split lip, and answered it by bloodying Devin's nose.

"But, darling, it looks like they've just gotten started."

"I mean it, Rafe." With a heavy sigh, Regan MacKade shifted the gurgling baby on her hip. "Break it up."

"Women," he muttered. But he would break it up his way, which was to dive into the fray, and get in a few licks of his own. Knowing he couldn't enjoy himself for long, he managed to shove Shane aside and sit on Devin.

"Stay out of this." Swiping at blood, Shane hauled himself to his knees. "It's between him and me."

"Maybe I will." Rafe was having quite a bit of trouble holding Devin down. To prove he meant to, he covered Devin's grimy face with the flat of his hand and gave it enough of a shove to have his head rapping against the concrete. "And maybe I want to play," he added. "What's it about?"

"Ask him." Already cooling off, Shane flexed his sore hand. "I was just talking to him, and he punched me."

"Well, I want to punch you half the time you're talking to me," Rafe said reasonably, and looked down to see that Devin's eyes were clearing. He hadn't meant to rap his brother's head quite that hard. "What were you talking to him about?"

"Stuff. Women."

Devin's vision was coming back, and so was his temper. He started to heave Rafe aside when Regan's firm, no-nonsense voice stopped him.

"That's just enough of this ridiculous behavior, Devin. You should be ashamed of yourself."

Still on top of him, Rafe looked down and grinned. "Yeah, Dev, you should be ashamed of yourself."

"Get the hell off me."

"You going to be a good boy?" With a laugh, Rafe leaned over and kissed him. He was quick, and agile, and sprang away before Devin could retaliate.

"A fine thing," Regan said from the doorway of the barn, making Devin think twice about jumping Shane again. She stood there in tailored slacks and a crisp spring blazer, a wide-eyed baby on her hip, a polished leather shoe tapping. "Wrestling in the barn like a couple of bad-tempered boys. Look at the two of you—you're filthy, bloody, and your clothes are torn."

"He started it." Wisely, Shane held back a laugh, and tried to look humble. "Honest, Regan, I was just defending myself."

"I'm not interested in who started it," Regan said regally, and deflated her brother-in-law with one snippy look. "I believe we were invited to dinner."

"Oh, yeah." Shane had forgotten about that. "We had a little trouble with a birthing. Breech calf. We just got finished."

"Oh." Instantly Regan was all concern. Tossing back a curtain of honey-brown hair, she hurried inside. "Is it all right?"

"Just dandy. Hey, Nate."

"No, you don't." Even as the cooing baby held out his arms to his uncle, Regan turned aside. "You're filthy. The two of you go clean up."

Devin eyed Shane narrowly, then hissed out a breath. "I felt like pounding somebody. You were available. You also have a big mouth."

Shane dabbed at the blood on his lip. "You sucker-punched me."

"So?"

"So I owe you one."

"That's it boys, kiss and make up."

When both Shane and Devin turned on Rafe, Regan gritted her teeth. "Stop right there. If nobody punches anyone else, I'll cook dinner."

"Good deal," Shane decided.

"But you're not coming in the kitchen until... What's that noise?"

"What noise?" Devin unclenched his ready fist and listened. The whimpering sound was soft, barely audible over little Nate's babbling. Homing in on it, he strode halfway down the barn and looked into another stall. "Looks like it's the day for birthing. Ethel's having her babies."

"Ethel." Like a frantic papa, Shane bolted down the barn, and all but fell into the stall beside his laboring pet. "Oh, honey, why didn't you call me? Jeez, she's already had two."

"Fred's probably out passing out cigars." At the entrance to the stall, Rafe leaned over and kissed his wife, then his son. "I know just how he feels."

Seeing the panic in Shane's eyes, Devin shook his head. They'd witnessed or assisted in countless births with the stock over the years, but that meant nothing now. This was Ethel, and she was as close to a true love as Shane had ever known. He stepped in, crouched down beside his brother.

"She's doing fine." He hooked an arm over Shane's shoulders.

"You think?"

"Sure. She's a MacKade, isn't she?" Devin glanced up at Regan and winked. "MacKade women are the best there is."

After the birthing, the cleaning up, the cooking and the celebrating of Fred and Ethel's six healthy puppies, Devin drove back to the office. He was too restless to stay at the farm. Though he had taken a long, soaking bath to soothe out the worst of the aches his scuffle with Shane had caused, he still wasn't able to fully relax.

He slowed down as he passed the inn, saw lights shining on the second and third floors. Grimly he punched the gas again and headed into town.

She wasn't going to forgive him easily, he thought. He wasn't going to forgive himself. He'd acted like a maniac. He'd been rough and demanding when she deserved, and should have expected, a gentle touch.

No wonder she'd looked at him as though he'd lost his mind, her eyes round in shock, her soft, pretty mouth trembling.

He'd make it up to her somehow, eventually. He knew how to bide his time, didn't he? He'd been waiting for her nearly half his life already.

* * *

Joe Dolin was also biding his time. His cell was dark, but he wasn't sleeping. He was planning. He knew most people thought he wasn't very smart, but he was going to show them, all of them, soon. He'd learned how to play the game, to say what the guards and the psychiatrists and the fat-faced warden wanted to hear. He'd learned how to act as they wanted him to act.

He could be humble. He could be repentant. He could be anything he had to be. As long as it got him out.

Devin MacKade thought he'd proved something, driving by the work site, flashing his badge. Oh, he owed Devin MacKade. Big-time. He hadn't forgotten the way Devin had come after him, had cuffed him and tossed him into a cell. No, he hadn't forgotten what he owed Devin. There would be payback.

But Cassie would come first, because he owed her most of all. Everything would have been fine if she'd stayed in her place. But she'd gone whining to MacKade, sniveling about their personal business.

A man had a right to punish his wife, to give her the back of his hand or let her feel his fist when she needed it. And Cassie had needed it a lot. She still did.

No fancy divorce papers changed that. She was his wife, his property, and he was going to be reminding her of that before too much longer.

Till death do us part, he thought, and smiled into the dark.

Chapter 4

Parade day was a tactical nightmare. That was to be expected. Over and above his usual reasons, Devin was looking forward to it, because it would keep him too busy to think about any personal problems.

The parade would kick off at twelve sharp—which meant anytime between noon and twelve-thirty—with the usual speeches at the square and the ceremonial laying of the wreath at the memorial.

As sheriff, he was required to be there, in full uniform. He could handle it. There were only a handful of days out of the year when he had to drag out the dress khakis and tie and shiny black shoes.

Of course, that meant dragging out the ironing board, as well, which he hated. It was the only domestic chore he truly despised, and the only one that jittered his nerves.

But by 8:00 a.m. he was pressed and dressed and out on the street. Already there were eager beavers claiming their spots, holding spaces along the curbs and sidewalks for others with lawn chairs and coolers.

Most of the storefronts and shops along the parade route were closed for the day, but he could count on Ed's being open for breakfast.

He sauntered down the sidewalk, knowing he had the best part of an hour before he had to worry about crowd control or making certain the concessionaires were in their proper places with their balloons and hot dogs and ice cream.

Summer had decided to make its debut on parade day. It was already hot, and he tugged irritably at his collar.

He imagined the tar on the street would be soft and melting by afternoon. He hoped the little girls who did their tumbles and cartwheels in their spangled uniforms were prepared.

He made a note to make certain there was plenty of water along the route for the marchers. He didn't want anybody fainting on him.

It might be a holiday, but Ed's was doing a brisk business. He could smell ham frying, coffee brewing. The scent reminded him that he'd been off his feed for the past couple of days.

After exchanging a few greetings with patrons in booths, he sidled up to the counter and took a stool.

"Sheriff." Ed winked at him. As usual, her rhinestone glasses were dangling on a pearl-studded chain against her scrawny chest. She wore a splattered apron, but beneath it she was ready for the celebration in a snug, midriff-baring top as red as her hair, and shorts that barely met the limits of the law.

She had bright blue shadow all the way up to her penciled brows, and her mouth was stop-sign red. Poppies dangled from her ears and were pinned to her apron.

Devin grinned at her. Only Edwina Crump could get away with an outfit like that.

"Ham and eggs, Ed, and keep the coffee coming."

"You got it, sweetie." Though she was old enough to be his mother, she fluffed her hair and flirted. "Don't you look handsome in your uniform!"

"I feel like an aging Boy Scout," he grumbled.

"One of my first beaus was a Boy Scout." She wiggled her brows as she took the clear plastic top off a plate of doughnuts and chose one for him. "He was surely prepared, let me tell you. On the house," she added, casting a sharp eye over her two scrambling waitresses.

She left Devin with his coffee and doughnut before heading back into the kitchen.

He tried not to brood, really. To keep himself sane, he set his clipboard on the counter and read over his notes and itinerary. A half hour later, he was doing some fine-tuning and trying to enjoy Ed's very excellent ham and eggs.

"Hi there, Sheriff. Locked anybody up lately?"

He swiveled on the stool and looked into the stunning and not altogether friendly face of his sister-in-law. Savannah MacKade always made a statement, Devin thought. When that lush siren's body sauntered into a room, men's hearts stopped. There was all that thick black hair falling past her shoulders, those almond-shaped eyes the color of sinful chocolate, and those ice-edged cheekbones against gold-dust skin.

And there was, Devin mused, all that attitude.

"As a matter of fact, no, not lately." He grinned at the boy beside her—his nephew, whether Savannah liked it or not. Tall for his age, and as dark and handsome as his mama, Bryan was sporting his baseball uniform and fielder's cap. "Riding in the parade today?"

"Yeah. Me and Con and the guys are riding in the coach's pickup. It'll be cool."

"Kind of early, aren't you?"

"We had some things to pick up," Savannah supplied. "Including Connor. We're on our way to get him as soon as Bryan here fills his stomach."

"I'm starving," the boy claimed and, eyeing the plate of doughnuts, he leaped onto the stool beside Devin.

"Hey, Ed, you got a starving boy out here."

"I'm coming." She slapped the swinging door of the kitchen open and strolled out. Her grin flashed at Bryan. "Well, it's my champ." As sponsor of the Antietam Cannons, Ed preened with pride. "Hell of a game Saturday." She saluted Savannah, leaned over the counter long enough to coo at the baby in the stroller, then fell into a deep and serious discussion with Bryan about food and baseball.

Devin didn't ask. He'd be damned if he would. He slid off the stool long enough to pick up his niece, then settled back down with the wide-eyed Layla on his lap.

Beneath the frilly sun hat, Layla's hair curled thick and dark. Her mouth—her mother's mouth, Devin mused—was serious as she watched him out of big eyes that were already easing from birth blue to MacKade green.

"Hello, beautiful." He bent over to kiss her, and was pleased to see that pretty mouth curve. "She smiled at me."

"Gas."

Devin looked up into Savannah's bland eyes. "The hell it is. She smiled at me. She loves me. Don't you, Layla? Don't you, darling?" He traced a finger over her hand until she gripped it. "She's got MacKade eyes."

"They're still changing," Savannah claimed. But she was softening. Despite the badge, and the fact that she tried to resist him, she grew fonder of Devin every day. "They might turn brown."

"Nah. MacKade eyes." He looked up again, smiled at her. "You're stuck with them. With us."

"Apparently."

His grin only widened. He knew she liked him, no matter how cool she tried to be. "Want a dough-nut?"

"Maybe." She gave up and slid onto a stool. "You don't have to hold her."

"I want to hold her. Where's Jared?"

"Doing some lawyer thing. He's going to meet us at the inn about nine-thirty."

"So, you haven't been by yet," Devin said casu-ally, very casually, as he shifted Layla to his shoulder and rubbed her back.

"No." Savannah bent down to take a cloth from the stroller and smoothed it over Devin's shoulder. "I nursed her right before we left. She's liable to spit up all over that pretty cop suit."

"Then I wouldn't have to wear it. You're just picking up Connor?"

"Mm-hmm..." With an expert's eye, Savannah selected her own doughnut. "Rafe and Regan are swinging by later to get Cassie and Emma. Shane's going to drive Jared in so we don't have so many cars when we head to the park for the picnic."

She glanced over, saw that her son was well on his way to demolishing the two doughnuts Ed had given him. "You angling for a ride?"

"No. I've got to take the cruiser so I can pretend I'm working."

"I didn't see you at the game Saturday."

"I swung by for a couple of innings." He'd spotted Cassie in the stands, and he hadn't wanted to make her uncomfortable.

"You didn't make it to Sunday dinner yesterday at the farm."

"Did you miss me?"

"Not particularly." But there was something in his eyes that wiped the sneer off her face. "Is something wrong, Devin?"

"No."

"Jared told me about Joe Dolin, the work release. It's bothering you."

"That's a mild term for it. I'm keeping my eye on him," he murmured, and turned his face into Layla's sweet-smelling neck to nuzzle.

"I'll bet you are," Savannah murmured. She brushed a hand over her daughter's head, then let it rest on Devin's shoulder in a gesture of affection and support that surprised both of them.

"Am I growing on you, Savannah?"

She let her hand drop, but the corners of her mouth quirked up. "Like you said, I'm stuck with you. Now give me my kid."

Devin settled Layla in her mother's arms, then kissed Savannah, firm and quick, on the mouth. "See you. See you, Bry," he added as he rose.

Bryan mumbled something, hampered by a mouthful of apple-filled doughnut.

"Damn MacKades," Savannah said under her breath. But she was smiling as she watched Devin stride away.

By noon, the town was bursting at the seams. People crowded the sidewalks and spilled over porches and front yards. Kids raced everywhere at once, and the bawling of fretful babies rose through the air like discordant music.

Several streets were barricaded to keep the parade route clear. Devin posted himself at the main intersection so that he could soothe travelers who had forgotten about parade day, or were from far enough out of town that they'd never heard of it.

He offered alternate routes, or invitations to park and join the festivities.

The two-way radio hitched to his belt belched and squawked with static or calls from deputies placed at distant points along the route.

Across the street from him, at the corner of the gas station, a clown sold colorful balloons. Half a block down, ice cream and snow cones were big sellers. They melted in the heat almost as soon as they were passed from hand to hand.

Devin looked at the wrappers, the spills, the bits of broken toys and balloons. Cleanup was going to be a bitch.

Then, in the distance, he heard the first of the marching bands approaching the square. The brassy music, the *click-clack* of booted feet, had his practical frame of mind shifting into the pleasures of his youth.

What the hell—there was just nothing like a parade.

"Officer! Officer!"

Resigned, Devin turned back to the barricade, where another car had pulled up. With one look, he summed up the middle-aged couple in the late-model sedan as hot, frazzled and annoyed.

"Yes, ma'am." He leaned down to the open window and gave them his best public-servant smile. "What can I do for you?"

"We have to get through here." The driver's irritated tone carried the flavor of the North that went with his Pennsylvania tags.

"I told you not to get off the highway, George. You just had to take the scenic route."

"Be quiet, Marsha. We have to get through," he said again.

"Well, now." Devin ran his hand over his chin. "The problem here is that we've got a parade going on." To prove it, the marching band let out a blare of trumpets, a boom of drums. Devin pitched his voice over the din. "We won't be able to open this road for another hour."

That sparked a heated domestic argument, demands, accusations. Devin kept the easy smile on his face. "Where y'all headed?"

"D.C."

"Well, I'll tell you what you can do, if you're in a hurry. You turn around and head straight up this road for about five miles. You're going to see signs to route 70. Take the eastbound. You'll hit the Washington Beltway—that's 495—in just about an hour."

"I told you not to get off the highway," Marsha said again.

George huffed. "How was I supposed to know some little one-horse town would block off the streets?"

"If you're not in a hurry," Devin continued, calm as a lake, "you can turn around and pull into that field where there's a sign for parking. It's free. We got a nice parade here." He glanced over as a junior majorette tossed up her baton and snagged it, to the forceful applause of the crowd. "I can give you a nice, pretty route into D.C."

"I haven't got time for any damn parade." Puffing out his cheeks, George slapped the sedan in reverse. Devin could hear them arguing as he jockeyed the car into a turn and headed off.

"Ain't that a shame..." Devin muttered, and turned, nearly knocking Cassie over. He grabbed her instinctively, then let her go as if her skin had burned his hands. "Sorry. Didn't see you."

"I thought I should wait until you'd finished being diplomatic."

"Yeah. George and Marsha don't know what they're missing."

Smiling, she watched the senior majorettes twirl and tumble. But in her mind she was still seeing Devin in his uniform. So competent and male. "I know. You must be hot. Would you like me to get you a drink?"

"No, I'm fine. Ah…" His tongue was in knots. He didn't know the last time he'd seen her in shorts. And over the years he'd done his best not to think about her legs. Now here they were, all long and smooth, showcased by neat little cuffed shorts the color of plums. "Where's Emma?"

"She's made friends with the little McCutcheon girl, Lucy. They're in her yard." It was easier to talk to him if she wasn't looking at him, so Cassie concentrated on the slow-moving convertible and its passenger, the waving and flouncily dressed current agriculture princess. "Are you angry with me, Devin?"

"No, of course not." He stared so hard at the princess that she flashed him a brilliant, hopeful smile, and a very personal wave. But it was Cassie he saw, looking shocked and delicate. And beautiful.

"You've flustered Julie," Cassie murmured, noting the exchange.

"Julie? Who's Julie?"

Her quick laugh surprised them both. Then they were staring at each other. "Are you sure you're not mad?"

"No. Yes. Yes, I'm sure." He jammed his hands into his pockets, where they would be safe. "Not at you. At me. Like I said, I was out of line the other day.''

"I didn't mind.''

The blare of the next band rang in his ears. He was sure he hadn't heard her correctly. "Excuse me?''

"I said I—'' She broke off when his two-way squawked.

"Sheriff. Sheriff, this here's Donnie. We got a little situation down to quadrant C. You there, Sheriff?''

"Quadrant C, my butt,'' Devin muttered. "He's at the elementary school. Watching too many *Dragnet* reruns.''

"I'll let you go,'' Cassie said quickly as he whipped out his two-way. "You're busy.''

"If you'd—'' He cursed again, because she was already hurrying through the cheering crowd. "Mac-Kade,'' he snapped into the receiver.

The little situation turned out to be a harmless brawl between overly loyal students at rival high schools. Devin broke it up, snarled at Donnie, then helped a mother deal with her terrified daughter, who had lost her breakfast over the idea of twirling her baton in public.

By the time the last marching boot clicked, the last flag waved and the last balloon drifted into the sky, he had to oversee the traffic headed for the park and the cleanup detail, and help a couple of weeping lost children find their way back to Mama.

He took his time cooling off under the stingy spray of his office shower, then gratefully retired his uniform until the next official event. By the time he made it to the park and snuck the cruiser in behind a trail of cars, the picnic, with its grilling food and boisterous games, was well under way.

There was softball, horseshoes, pitching contests, egg-throwing contests, three-legged races. He saw Shane nuzzling Frannie Spader, the curvy redhead he had so generously offered Devin a few days before.

There was Rafe, stepping up to bat, and Jared winding up to pitch. Regan and Savannah were spread out in the shade with their babies.

There were dogs and kids, big-bellied men sitting in lawn chairs, discussing sports and politics, old women fanning themselves and laughing. There was Cy, the town mayor, looking ridiculous as always, sporting a pair of violently checkered Bermuda shorts that still exposed far too much of his hairy legs.

Mrs. Metz was shouting encouragement to her grandchildren, gnawing on a chicken leg and gossiping with Miss Sarah Jane.

Good God, Devin thought, he really loved them. All of them.

He wandered over the grass, stopping here and there to chat or listen to a complaint or a snippet of news. With his hands tucked in his back pockets he watched solemnly with old Mr. Wineburger as horseshoes were tossed and clanged against the pole.

He was debating different techniques of horseshoe pitching when Emma came up quietly and held out her arms. He picked her up, settled her on his hip while Wineburger wheezed out opinions. But Devin's mind had begun to wander.

Little Emma smelled like sunshine and was as tiny as a fairy. But she was nearly seven now, he recalled with a jolt. Soon she wouldn't want to be picked up and held. She would, like the young girls he saw over at the edge of the field, be flirting with young boys, want to be left alone to experiment with being female.

He sighed and gave her a quick squeeze.

"How come you're sad?" she wanted to know.

"I'm not. I'm just thinking that you're growing up on me. How about a snow cone?"

"Okay. A purple one."

"A purple one," he agreed, and set her down. Hands linked, they walked toward the machine manned by the American Legion. He bought two, then settled down with her on the grass to watch the softball match.

"Come on, Dev!" From his position at second, Rafe shouted to his brother. "Batter up!"

"I'm not moving. I've got me a pretty girl here," he shouted back.

"Mama says I'm pretty, too."

He smiled at Emma, ruffled her hair. "That's because you are."

"Mama's pretty."

"She sure is."

Emma cuddled closer, knowing his arm would come around her, just the way she liked it. "She hardly ever cries anymore." In her innocence, she licked at the snow cone and didn't notice the way Devin's arm went taut. "She used to cry all the time, at nighttime. But now she doesn't."

"That's good" was all Devin could manage.

"And we got to have Ed the kitten, and a brand-new house, and nobody yells and breaks things or hits Mama now. Connor gets to play baseball and write stories, and I can have Lucy come right to my room to play. I've got pretty curtains, too, with puppies on them. And new shoes."

She wiggled her pink sneakers for Devin's benefit.

"They're very nice."

"It's 'cause you made him go away, the bad man. Connor said you arrested him and sent him to jail and now he can't hit Mama and make her cry." She looked up at him, her mouth circled with sticky purple, her eyes wide and clear. "I love you."

"Oh, Emma..." Undone, he lowered his brow to her soft golden curls. "I love you, too. You're my best girl."

"I know." She puckered her purple lips and planted a sticky kiss on his cheek. "I'm going to get Lucy now. She's my very best friend." She got to her feet, smiled her mother's soft smile. "Thank you for the snow cone."

"You're welcome."

He watched her dance off, pretty as a pixie, then rubbed his hands over his face. It was hard enough being in love with the mother. What the hell was he going to do with this need for the child?

Was he going to have to settle—always—for protecting, for watching over, for being the dependable friend, the favored honorary uncle?

He was getting damn sick of it, of holding in, of holding back.

This time, when Rafe called out, Devin got to his feet. Yeah, he thought, he'd batter up, all right. God knew he needed to hit something.

There was something intrinsically satisfying about smacking a little white ball with a slim wooden bat. It was the connection, the way the power of it sang up the arms. It was the sound, the solid crack, the whoosh of air, the rising cheers as the ball lifted.

He was feeling human by the time he rounded third and headed for home. More than human, since it turned out to be Shane guarding the plate. His lips peeled back in a feral grin matching his brother's as he went into a hard, bruising headfirst slide.

There was the brutal collision of flesh and bone, the swirl of choking dust, the hysterical screams of fans and teammates. He heard Shane grunt as his elbow whipped around to catch his brother in the ribs, beside the padded catcher's vest. He saw stars as some bony part, probably Shane's knee, caught him beside the ear.

But what he heard over it all was the glorifying call of "Safe!"

"I'll be damned." Shane had managed to hold on to the ball that Jared had bulleted to him, even after the nasty collision. "I tagged the sucker," Shane insisted, waving the ball for emphasis.

Cy, the umpire, hung tough. "You weren't on the plate, Shane. Devin was. You didn't get the tag in time."

That, of course, was tantamount to a declaration of war.

From the sidelines, Savannah watched the very polished attorney Jared MacKade go nose-to-nose with the town's mayor, while her brothers-in-law shouted at each other, and anyone else who happened to get in the way.

"I love picnics," Savannah commented.

"Mmm... Me too." Regan stretched her arms. "They're so relaxing." She smiled up at Cassie, who stepped under the shade with them. "Don't worry," she said, noting the way Cassie hugged her arms. "They won't hurt each other. Very much."

"I know." She tried not to be so poor-spirited. The MacKades were always yelling. But she hugged herself tighter when she saw Connor and Bryan race up to get a piece of the action.

"Don't worry," Regan said again.

"No, I won't."

It was good, wasn't it, that Connor could race and shout that way? He'd been too quiet for too long. Too worried, she thought guiltily. He was coming into himself more and more every day. And if picking sides over a baseball call made him happy, then no, she wouldn't let herself worry.

It was over soon enough, with vows of revenge and retaliation. She watched Bryan do a victory boogie, then nag until he was allowed up to the plate. Devin picked up a mitt, bent over and said something that had Connor goggling with pleasure. Her son raced into the outfield and joined the game.

"He's awfully good with children," Cassie murmured. "Devin," she added.

"Every time he comes by the house, he has Nate on his hip the minute he steps through the door." Regan smiled down at her son, who was busy chewing on a bright red teething ring. "He's bleeding."

Alarmed, Cassie looked down at Nate. "Where?"

"No, I meant Devin. His mouth's bleeding. Anyone got a tissue?"

"I do." Cassie pulled one out of her pocket.

As she hurried over to where Devin was walking to the outfield, Regan grinned. "She hasn't figured it out yet, has she?"

"Nope." Savannah leaned back against the tree. Layla was napping, and that seemed like a wonderful idea. "He's going to have to do something a little more obvious for her to realize he's crazy about her."

"He's the only MacKade I know who moves slow."

Savannah arched a brow before she closed her eyes. "I'll bet he moves fast enough when the time comes. Cassie won't have a chance."

"No," Regan said softly. "She'll have the best chance of her life."

Out of breath from the effort of catching up with his long strides, Cassie called out, "Devin! Wait a minute!"

He glanced around, saw her rushing after him and did what he'd trained himself to do. He put his hands in his pockets. "What?"

"Your mouth. Gosh, you must be all leg," she managed, puffing, when she stopped in front of him.

"My mouth?"

"It's bleeding." In practiced maternal gestures, she dabbed at the corner of his mouth. "I saw you dive headfirst into Shane. I had to close my eyes. You're lucky you only cut your lip doing something that crazy. It's only a game."

"It's baseball," he reminded her, and struggled not to groan as her fingers gently soothed the wound he hadn't even been aware of. "I got the run."

"Yes, I know. I'm learning all the rules and terms. RBIs and ERAs. Connor's so excited about playing. It was sweet of you to let him go into left field."

"Right. Right field," Devin managed as his heart jitterbugged in his chest. He kept his hands balled into fists in his pockets. "Cassie, I'm fine."

It was the tone, the sharp impatience in it, that had her stopping. "You are mad at me."

"I'm not mad at you. Damn it, I'm not mad. Look." Frustrated beyond belief, he snatched the blood-spotted tissue from her hands. "What's this?"

"It's blood. I told you your mouth—"

"Blood," he said, interrupting her. "That's what I've got in my veins. Blood, not ice water. So if you're going to keep leaning up against me and putting your hands on my face, I—" He cut himself off, clenched his teeth. "I'm not mad," he said, more calmly. "I need to take a walk."

Cassie gnawed at her lip as he strode away into the little grove of trees that lined the east side of the park. The idea of losing his friendship gave her all the courage she needed to follow him.

He stopped, turned, and the heat in his eyes was like an arrow in her heart. "I'm sorry," she said quickly. "I'm sorry, Devin."

"Don't say you're sorry to me, Cassie, you have nothing to apologize for." Where the hell was everybody? he asked himself. Why weren't there people in the grove? He couldn't risk being alone with her now, when he didn't have himself under complete control. "Go on back, Cassie. Go on, now."

She started to. It was second nature for her to do as she was told. But she couldn't, not this time. Not when it was so important. "If you're not mad, then you're upset. I don't want to be the cause of that."

It was hard, almost terrifying, to step forward, when there was still temper simmering in his eyes. She knew he wouldn't hurt her, of course she knew, but there was a part of her that couldn't be entirely sure. But for Devin she'd risk it.

"It's because I kissed you," she blurted out. "I didn't mean anything by it."

The temper drained from his eyes. There were blank now, carefully blank. "I know you didn't."

"You kissed me back." Her heart was pounding so hard she could barely hear herself speak. "You said you were angry with yourself for doing it, but I don't want you to be. I didn't mind."

"You didn't mind," he repeated, spacing out the words. "Okay. We'll put it aside. Go on back now."

"Why did you kiss me like that?" The words ended on a whisper as her courage began to flag.

"Like I told you, you caught me off guard." When she only continued to stare at him with those big, soft eyes, he felt something snap. "Damn it, what do you want from me? I apologized, didn't I? I said it wouldn't happen again. I'm trying to stay away from you, and it's killing me. I've waited to kiss you for twelve years, and when I do I practically eat you alive. I didn't mean to hurt you."

Her knees were starting to shake, but it didn't feel like fear. She knew fear well enough to recognize it. But whatever this was that was working through her was unfamiliar.

"You didn't hurt me." She had to swallow. "I didn't mind. I don't mind."

He was trying to get a bead on her, but wasn't sure of his aim. "I want to kiss you again."

"I don't mind," she repeated, because it was the best she could do.

She didn't move as he stepped toward her, had no idea if she should touch him. She would have liked to run her hands up those arms, they were so strong. But she wasn't sure.

Then she didn't have to worry, or think, or try to guess. He laid his hands on her cheeks, framing her face, and lowered his mouth to hers, so gently, so patiently.

Her heart fluttered, and the sensation was sweet, like something flying silently out of a cage when the door has been opened unexpectedly. When he drew her closer, just a little closer, she thought she floated toward him. Her lips parted on a sigh of quiet wonder.

This was what he meant to do, always. Show her tenderness and care. Let himself slide into her slowly, gently. The dappled shade was perfect, sweetened by the call of birds and the tang of wildflowers.

This was what he'd meant to do, he thought hazily, and deepened the kiss with patient skill until she sighed again.

And all the years he'd waited and wanted seemed like minutes, now that she was here, with him.

The sound of the shouts and laughter from the field beyond was like the buzz of happy bees in her head. She didn't realize she'd lifted her hands, curled them around his wrists, until she felt the strong quick beat of his pulse against her fingers. She held on as lovely colors began to revolve in her head, as the kiss went on and on, spinning out time.

He didn't let her go until her hands had slipped weakly from his wrists to fall to her sides.

Her eyes were still closed when he lifted his head, when he moved his hands from her face to her shoulders. As he watched, she pressed her lips together, as if to draw in that last taste, and savor it.

"Cassie."

She opened her eyes, and they were heavy and clouded and confused. "I don't know what to say now." Yes, she did, she realized. "Will you kiss me again?"

Twelve years of repression kept him from groaning out loud. "Not just this minute," he said, and held her at arm's length. Any closer, and he might just toss her over his shoulder and carry her off behind some handy rock. He wasn't sure either of them was ready for that. "I figure we ought to spread it out a little."

"No one's ever kissed me like that. Made me feel like this."

"Cassie." The words had his libido growing fangs. Snapping down on it, he took her hand. "Let's go back. I . . . haven't had lunch."

"Oh, you must be starving."

"Right." He could almost laugh at himself as he pulled her back onto the field.

Chapter 5

"I really appreciate this, Cassie." Regan tucked a giggling Nate into his portable swing, then bent over to kiss him as he bounced gleefully. "With out-of-town clients coming into the shop this morning, I just can't keep him with me. And Rafe's got two crews to supervise."

"It's a real hardship," Cassie said from the sink. "I can't think of anything more annoying than having to play with the baby."

"He is wonderful, isn't he? I can't believe he's already five months old." When she cranked up the music on the swing, Nate began to kick his feet in delight. "I nursed him an hour ago, and I've got plenty of bottles here, and diapers, and two changes of clothes, and—"

"Regan, I know what to do with a baby."

"Of course you do." Grinning foolishly at Nate, Regan swept her hair back. "It's just that I know you're so busy with the inn."

"You and Rafe are slave drivers, it's true, but I'm learning to bear up."

Amused, Regan cocked her head. "You're joking, and you're smiling, and I'm pretty sure I heard you singing when I came in."

"I'm happy." Cassie loaded plates into the dishwasher. The breakfast hour was over, and the guests were either gone or relaxing in their rooms. "I didn't know I could be this happy. This is the most wonderful house in the world."

Regan handed Nate a ring of colorful plastic to jiggle. "So working here makes you happy?"

"Absolutely. Not that I wasn't happy working for Ed, but... I love living here, Regan." She beamed at the view from the window. "The kids love living here."

Regan ran her tongue around her teeth. "And that's why you were singing?"

Cassie bent over a little farther, busied herself arranging dishes. "Actually, there is something else. I guess you've got to go open the shop."

"I've got a few minutes. One of the perks of running my own business."

If there was anyone she could talk to, it was Regan. Cassie straightened, took a deep breath. "Devin—it's about Devin. That is, I'm probably making too much of it. Or not making enough of it. It's just, well... Do you want some coffee?"

"Cassie."

"He kissed me," she blurted out, then slapped a hand to her mouth when a laugh bubbled out. "I mean, *kissed* me. Not like Rafe kisses me, or Shane or Jared. I mean, like . . . My hands are sweating."

"It's about time," Regan said, with feeling. "I thought he'd never get to it."

"You're not surprised."

"Cassie, the man would crawl naked over hot coals for you." She decided she would have some coffee, and walked over to the stove to pour it herself. "So, how was it?"

Regan's statement had Cassie running a nervous hand through her hair. "How was what?"

With a chuckle, Regan sipped and leaned back against the counter. "I have to figure that he has more in common with Rafe than a quick temper and great looks. So it must have been a pretty terrific kiss."

"It was at the picnic, two days ago. My head's still buzzing."

"Yep. That's a MacKade for you. What are you going to do about it?"

"I don't know what to do." Brow creased, Cassie picked up a damp rag and began to wipe the counter. "Regan, I started going with Joe before I was sixteen. I've never been with anyone else."

"Oh." Regan pursed her lips. "I see. Well, it would be only natural to be a little nervous over the idea that you might be heading toward a physical relationship."

Because her palms were indeed damp, Cassie set down the cloth and rubbed them on her apron. "I don't like sex," she said flatly, rattling dishes again so that she didn't note the lift of Regan's brow or the concern in her friend's eyes. "I'm not any good at it, and I just don't like it, anyway."

"Cassie, I know the counseling helped you."

"Yes, it did, and I'm grateful for you persuading me to go. I feel better about myself, and I'm more confident about a lot of things. I know I didn't deserve to be abused, that I didn't cause it, and that I did the right thing by getting out." She let out a breath. "This is a different matter. Not all women are built to enjoy sex. I've read about it. Anyway," she continued before Regan could comment, "I'm getting ahead of myself. But I'm not stupid, Regan. I know that Devin has needs, and I'm prepared to meet them."

"That is stupid," Regan snapped. "Making love is not supposed to be a chore like—like..." Flustered, she gestured to the sink. "Like doing the damn dishes."

"I didn't mean it that way." Because Regan was her friend, she smiled. "What I meant was that I care for Devin. I always have. This is a different level. I didn't know he was attracted to me. I'm so flattered."

Regan's response to that was a muttered curse that only made Cassie's smile widen.

"Well, I am. He's so beautiful, and he's kind. I know he won't hurt me."

"No," Regan said quietly. "He wouldn't hurt you." But, she thought, would you hurt him?

"Kissing him was lovely, and I think having sex with him would be nice."

Wisely, Regan covered her cough with a sip of coffee. If Devin was anything like Rafe, *nice* was hardly the word. "Has he asked you to bed?"

"No. He wouldn't even kiss me again when I asked him to. That's what I wanted to ask you about. How do I go about letting him know I don't mind being with him—that way?"

It was a tribute to her willpower that Regan didn't goggle. Carefully she set the coffee cup aside. "This goes against the grain for me, Cassie, against every feminist cell in my body, but I have to trust my instincts here, and go with what I know about you and about Devin. I'm going to advise you to let him set the pace, at least initially. Take your cues from him. Just relax and enjoy the ride. I think you can count on him to get you both where you want to go. When you're ready, Cassie. It's important to think of yourself, too, not just Devin."

"So I really shouldn't do anything?"

"Do what seems right to you. And do this—don't compare him with Joe. And don't compare the woman who lived with Joe with the woman you are now. I think you're in for a few surprises."

"I've already had one." Cassie touched a fingertip to her lips. "It was wonderful."

"Good. Keep an open mind." She gave Cassie a quick kiss, bent down to fuss over Nate one last time. "And, Cass, I really wouldn't mind if you sort of kept me up-to-date with the progress."

By mid-afternoon, Cassie had finished the guest rooms, and the laundry, and had Nate tucked in a portable crib in Emma's room for a nap. She'd slipped a chicken in the oven to roast and was giving some thought to tackling the mending when she heard the quick rap on her door.

Her heart did a little flip at the hope that it might be Devin stopping by. But settled again when she saw her mother through the screen.

"Hello, Mama." Dutifully Cassie opened the door and pecked her mother's dry cheek. "It's nice to see you. I've just made some iced tea, and I have some nice cherry cobbler."

"You know I don't eat sweets in the middle of the day." Constance Connor scanned the living area of her daughter's quarters. She wrinkled her nose at the cat that curled under the table. Animals belonged outside.

The curtains were drawn back, which would surely fade the upholstery with that strong sunlight. But it was neat. She'd taught her daughter to be neat.

After all, cleanliness was next to godliness.

Still, she didn't care for the bright colors, or all the folderols sitting about. It was showy. She sniffed to indicate her disapproval and sat down on one of the living room chairs, her back broomstick-straight.

"I'll say again, it's a poor choice for you to live in a man's house who isn't your husband."

It was an old argument, and Cassie answered by rote. "I lived in Mr. Halleran's house for nearly ten years."

"And paid good rent."

"I earn my keep here. What's the difference?"

"You know very well the difference, so I'll not mention it again."

Until the next time, Cassie thought wearily. "Would you like some iced tea, Mama?"

"I can get through an hour without sipping or snacking." Constance set her purse firmly on her lap, crossed her ankles above her sensible shoes. "Sit down, Cassandra. The children are in school, I take it."

"Yes. They're doing very well. They'll be home in about an hour. I hope you'll stay and see them."

"It's you I've come to see." She unsnapped her bag with fingers adorned with only a thin gold band. There was no glint to it, no shine. As, Cassie thought, there had been no glint or shine to her parents' marriage. She often thought, after a visit with her mother, that her father had died simply to escape it.

But she said nothing, waiting as her mother drew out an envelope. She didn't have to see the handwriting to know who it was from.

"This is the latest letter I received from your husband. It came in this morning's mail." Constance held it out. "I want you to read it."

Cassie folded her hands in her lap, linked her fingers. "No."

Eyes narrowed with righteous anger, Constance studied her daughter. "Cassandra, you will read this letter."

"No, ma'am, I won't. He's not my husband."

Constance's thin, pale face went dark with temper. "You took vows before God."

"And I've broken them." It was hard, so hard, to keep her voice and hands from trembling, to keep her eyes level.

"You take pride in that? You should be ashamed."

"No, not pride. But you can't make me sorry for breaking them, Mama. Joe broke them long before I did."

She refused to look at the letter, refused to feel this bitter anger, that even so small a part of him had come into her home. Instead, she kept her eyes on her mother's face.

"Love, honor, cherish. Did he love me, Mama, when he beat me? Did he honor me when he used his fists on me? Did he cherish me when he raped me?"

"You will not speak that way about your husband."

"I came to you when I had nowhere to go, when he'd hurt me so badly I could hardly walk, when my children were terrorized. And you sent me away."

"Your place was at home, making the best of your marriage."

"I made the best of it for ten years, and it nearly killed me. You should have been there for me, Mama. You should have stood up for me."

"I stood up for what was right." Constance's mouth was a thin line. "If you forced him to discipline you—"

"Discipline me!" Stunned, even after all the time that had passed, Cassie leaped to her feet. "He had no right to *discipline* me. I was his wife, not his dog. And not even a dog deserved to be treated the way I was. He would have disciplined me to death, if I hadn't finally found the courage to do something about it. Would that have satisfied you, Mama? I'd have kept my vows then. Till death do us part."

"You're overdramatizing. And whatever happened before is done. He's seen his mistakes. It was the drink, the women who tempted him. He's asking for your forgiveness, and hopes that you will keep your vows, as he intends to."

"He can't have my forgiveness, and he can't have me. How can you do this to me? I'm your daughter, your only child." Cassie's eyes were no longer haunted, but steely. "How can you take the side of a man who hurt me and betrayed me and made my life a misery? Don't you want me to be happy?"

"I want you to do what's expected of you. I expect you to do as you're told."

"Yes, that's all you ever wanted from me. To do what I was told, to be what you expected me to be. Why do you think I married him, Mama?"

Cassie couldn't believe the words were coming out of her mouth, but they wouldn't be stopped. Just as the emotions that pushed them from her heart to her throat and through her lips wouldn't be stopped.

"It was to get away from you, to get out of that house, where nobody ever laughed, nobody ever showed any affection."

"You had a good home." This time it was Constance whose voice trembled. "You had a decent Christian upbringing."

"No, I didn't. There's nothing decent or Christian about a house where there's no love. My children won't be raised that way, not anymore." Cassie spoke calmly now, amazed that she could, fascinated that she felt nothing at all. "You're my mother, and I'll give you all the respect that I can. All I'm asking is for you to give me the same. I don't want you corresponding with Joe anymore."

Constance got to her feet. "You would dare tell me what to do?"

"Will you stop writing him, Mama? Will you stop writing the prison authorities?"

"I will not."

"Then you're not welcome in my home. We have nothing else to say to each other."

Staggered, Constance could only stare. "You'll come to your senses."

"I have come to them. Goodbye, Mama."

Cassie walked to the door and held it open. She stiffened when Constance swept by. And then the trembling began.

Slowly, unsure of her footing, Cassie walked to the table. She braced herself on it as she lowered herself into a chair. Wrapping her arms tight around her body, she began to rock.

She was still sitting there when Devin came to the door, ten minutes later. He started to give a friendly rap on the wooden slat of the screen. But then he saw her, saw the way her shoulders were hunched and curled and the quick, monotonous rocking of her body, as if she were trying to still something inside herself. Or comfort it.

He'd seen her like that before, sitting in his office with her face battered. All he knew was that she was hurt, and he was through the door like a bullet.

"Cassie."

She sprang to her feet. He saw alarm mix with the hurt. Even as he reached out, she scooted back, out of his way.

"Devin, I didn't hear you come up. I was— I should—" Her mind raced for excuses, for the barrier of appearances. As always. Pale with grief, her eyes swimming with it, she stared at him. Then she began to move quickly. "Let me get you some iced tea. It's fresh." She was hurrying for glasses, for the pitcher, her movements jerky. "I've got some cobbler. I just made it this morning."

She jolted like a spring when his hands came down on her shoulders, and the glass she had just filled smashed on the tiles. The cat that had been napping under the table took off in a blur of fur.

"Oh, God, look what I've done." Her breathing hitched, and the feeling in her chest tightened. She couldn't stop it. "I have to— I have to—"

"Leave it." He struggled to keep his voice easy as he turned her to face him. She was shaking hard, trying to pull back. *Not this time* was all he could think. *Not this time.* "Come here," he murmured. "Come on now."

The instant he drew her into his arms, the dam broke. She wept against his shoulder, the fast, hot tears soaking his shirt. He kissed her hair, stroked her back. "Tell me. Tell me what's wrong, so I can help."

It wasn't coherent, nor was it complete, but he understood the gist when she stuttered out words between sobs. Bitter fury curled inside him as he soothed her, kissing her wet cheeks.

"You did what you had to do. You did what was right."

"She's my mother." Cassie lifted her ravaged face to his. "I sent her away. I turned my mother away."

"Who turned who away, Cass?"

Her breath sobbed out again, and her hands balled into fists on his shoulders. "It's not right."

"Get away from her." The screen door slammed as Connor burst through it. His own hands were fisted, and his face was flushed with fury, taut with violence. All he saw was a man holding his mother, and his mother crying. "If you touch her I'll kill you."

"Connor!" Shock had Cassie's voice ringing sharp. Was this her baby, with his fists raised and his eyes fierce? She caught a glimpse of Emma at the door, her frightened face pressed to the screen. "Don't speak that way to Sheriff MacKade."

Every cell on alert, Connor stepped forward. "Take your hands off my mother."

Intrigued, Devin merely lifted a brow and let his arms fall to his sides.

"I said not to speak that way," Cassie began.

"He was hurting you. He made you cry." Connor bared his teeth, a ten-year-old warrior. "He better leave right now."

"He wasn't hurting me." Though she was shaken to the core, Cassie stepped between them. "I was upset—Grandma upset me—and Sheriff MacKade was helping to make me feel better. I want you to apologize, this minute."

Devin saw the boy's arms drop, and knew when the angry flush on Connor's cheeks turned to shame. With his eyes on the boy, he laid a hand on Cassie's shoulder.

"I'd like to talk to Connor. Alone." Anticipating her protest, he gave Cassie's shoulder a quick squeeze. "Cass, the baby's crying. Why don't you and Emma go see to him?"

"Nate. I forgot." At her wit's end, Cassie dragged a hand through her hair.

"Why don't you go on?" Devin said, giving her a gentle nudge. "Con and I are going to take a walk."

"All right. Come on, Emma, Nate's crying." But she took a deep breath as she held out a hand for her daughter. "I expect you to apologize, Connor. You understand?"

"Yes, ma'am." With his chin on his chest, Connor turned to go outside.

He knew what was coming. He was going to get whipped. His father had always done the hitting away from the house, away where his mother couldn't see and wouldn't know. He'd get a beating now for sure, and it would be worse than anything his father had ever done to him. Because he'd tried to do what was right, and he'd been wrong.

Devin said nothing at all, just walked with the boy across the lawn, toward the woods that bordered it. He chose the path without thinking. The woods were as familiar to him as the town, as his own home, as his own mind. Beside him, Connor walked stiffly, his head drooped in shame, his back braced.

Because he knew he had to gauge his timing, and his moves, Devin resisted the urge to drape his arm over those thin little shoulders. Instead, he led the way down a path and stopped at the cluster of rocks where two soldiers had once met and doomed each other.

He sat, and the boy stood rigid and waiting.

"I'm awfully proud of you, Connor."

The words—the last he'd expected to hear—had the boy's head whipping up. "Sir?"

Casually Devin took out a cigarette—the first of a very long day. "I have to tell you, it's a relief to me. I worry about your mother some. She's had a bad time of it. Knowing you're there to look after things, makes my mind a lot easier."

Connor's confusion was too huge for him to feel any pride. He stared at Devin, his eyes still wary. "I—I sassed you."

"I don't think so."

"You're not going to hit me?"

Devin's hand stiffened, hesitated. Very slowly he tossed the barely smoked cigarette on the ground and crushed it under his heel. As he would have liked to crush Joe Dolin.

"I'm never going to raise my hand to you, not today, not any day." He spoke deliberately, his eyes level with Connor's, as a man would speak to another man. "I'm never going to raise it to your mama or to your sister." But he held out that hand, and waited. "I'm giving you my word, Connor," he said, when the boy simply stared at the hand being offered. "I'd be grateful if you'd take it."

Dumbfounded, Connor put his hand in Devin's. "Yes, sir."

Devin gave the hand a little squeeze, tugged the boy a little closer. And grinned. "You'd have torn right into me, wouldn't you?"

"I'd have tried." The emotions swirling inside Connor were frightening. Most of all, he was afraid he would cry now and show Devin he was just a stupid little boy after all. "I never helped her before. I never did anything."

"It wasn't your fault, Connor."

"I never did anything," Connor repeated. "He hit her all the time, Sheriff. All the time."

"I know."

"No, you don't. You only know about when one of the neighbors would call you, or when he'd get so drunk he'd hit her someplace where it would show. But there was more. It was worse."

Devin nodded. There was nothing else he could do. And drew the boy down on the rocks beside him. "He hit you, too."

"When she couldn't see." Bravery forgotten, Connor pressed his face into Devin's side. "When she didn't know."

Devin stared off into the trees, eaten away by a useless anger at what he hadn't been able to prevent. "Emma?"

"No, sir. He never paid much attention to Emma, because she was just a girl. Don't tell Mama. Please don't tell her he hit me. She'd just feel bad."

"I won't."

"I hate him. I'd kill him if I could."

"I know how you feel." When the boy shook his head, Devin drew him back, looked deep into his eyes.

"I do know. I'm going to tell you something. I used to fight a lot."

"I know." Connor sniffled, but was profoundly grateful he'd controlled the tears. "People talk about it."

"Yeah, I know they do. I used to like it, and I used to think there were lots of people I wanted to rip into. Sometimes I had reason for it, sometimes I didn't. Anyway, I had to learn to take a step back. It's important, that step. Now, you figure you owe your father some grief—"

"Don't call him that," Connor snapped out, then flushed darkly. "Sir."

"All right. I figure you owe him some, too. But you've got to take that step back. Let the law handle it."

"I'm not ever going to let him or anybody hurt her again."

"I'm with you there." Studying Connor's determined face, he decided the boy deserved to know the situation. "I'm going to give it to you straight, okay?"

"Yes, sir."

"Your grandma got your mama real upset today."

"She wants him to come back. It's never going to happen. I won't let it happen."

"Your mama feels the same way, and that's why she sent your grandma away. That was hard for her, real hard, Connor, but she did it."

"You were helping her. I'm sorry I—"

"Don't apologize," Devin said quickly. "I mean it. I know Cassie thinks you should, but we know how things stand. You did exactly right, Connor. I'd have done the same.''

No compliment he'd ever received, no praise from a teacher, no high-five from a teammate, had ever meant more. He had done what Sheriff MacKade would do.

"I'm glad you want to help her. I'll do anything you want me to do.''

That kind of trust, Devin thought, was worth more than gold. "I need to tell you that they've given Joe work release.''

Connor's face tightened up. "I know about it. Kids at school say things.''

"They giving you a rough time?''

He moved a shoulder. "Not as much as they used to.''

Learning to handle yourself, Devin thought with an astonishing sense of pride. "What I want is for you not to worry too much, but more, I want you to keep your eyes open. You're smart, and you notice things. That's why you write good stories.''

Connor wriggled with pleasure. "I like to write.''

"I know. And you know how to look at things, how to watch. So I know you're going to watch out for your family. If you see something, hear something, even feel something that doesn't sit right, I want you to come to me. I want your word on that.''

"Yes, sir.''

"Do you have to call me sir all the time? It makes me feel creaky.''

Connor flushed, and grinned. "I'm supposed to. It's like a rule.''

"I know all about rules." Devin decided they could deal with that little matter later. "A man would be lucky to have you for a son, Connor."

"I don't ever want to have a father again."

The hand that had lifted toward Connor's shoulder stiffened. Biting back a sigh, Devin ordered it to relax. "Then I'll say a man would be lucky to have you for a friend. Are we square here?"

"Yes, sir."

There were those eyes again, Devin thought, filled with trust. "Your mama's probably worried you're beating me up." When Connor giggled at the idea, Devin ruffled his hair. "You go on back now and tell her we straightened it all out. I'll talk to her later."

"Yes, sir." He scrambled off the rocks, then had to bite his lip to spark that last bit of courage. "Can I come to your office sometime, and watch you work?"

"Sure."

"I wouldn't get in the way. I'd just—" Connor tumbled over his own words and skidded to a halt. "I can?"

"Sure you can. Anytime. It's mostly boring."

"It couldn't be," Connor said with giddy pleasure. "Thanks, Sheriff. Thanks for everything."

Devin watched the boy race off, then settled back. He wished briefly for a cigarette before reminding himself he was quitting. Then he reminded himself that sooner or later he intended to have those two children, and maybe another on the way.

Connor didn't want another father, and that would be a tough one. So, Devin mused, he'd just have to find the right path to take, and step carefully.

The first step, of course, was Cassie. One step, then the next. Direction always took you somewhere. If he was careful, she would be taking those steps with him.

Chapter 6

It was supposed to be Devin's day off, but he spent two hours in the morning dealing with a small crisis at the high school. The smoke bomb had failed in its mission. When it landed in the girl's locker room, it hadn't put out much of a cloud, and, more important, hadn't made the girls come rushing out screaming in their underwear.

The one he'd put together a short lifetime ago had had far more satisfying results. Not that he'd mentioned that particular incident to the two offenders he collared.

Once he had it under control, and the juvenile chemists shaking in their basketball shoes, he headed straight for the inn.

He had a surprise for Cassie, one he hoped would

make her smile. And one he hoped would ease the way into that next step.

He supposed he had an unfair advantage. He knew her so well, had watched and observed for years. He knew every expression of her face, every gesture of her hands. He knew her weaknesses and her strengths.

She knew him, he thought, but not in the same way, or in the same detail. She'd been too busy surviving to notice. If she had noticed, she would have been able to see that he was in love with her.

It was just as well she didn't see. Not until he'd finished laying the foundation. He could take his time about that, Devin mused as he turned up the lane toward the inn. But once he had that foundation in place and solid, he was going to move fast.

Twelve years was a damn long time to wait.

Because there was a car parked in one of the guest slots, he opted to go into the inn first. He was delighted to find her there, fully occupied with two snowy-haired women.

She'd forgotten to take her apron off. The new arrivals had come unexpectedly, and they had wanted a full tour, and the history of the inn. Cassie was grateful she'd finished the breakfast dishes, even though she'd been caught in the middle of vacuuming.

The two women were sisters, both widowed, and were eager to hear about the Barlow legend. Cassie led them back down the stairs after the tour of the second floor, and was well into her spiel when Devin walked in.

"... the bloodiest single day of the Civil War. The Antietam battlefield is one of the most pristine parks in the country. The visitors' center is only four miles from here, and very informative. You'll find— Oh, hello, Devin.''

''Don't let me interrupt. Ladies.''

''Mrs. Berman, Mrs. Cox, this is Sheriff Mac-Kade.''

''Sheriff.'' Mrs. Cox adjusted her glasses and beamed through the lenses. ''How exciting.''

''Antietam's a quiet town,'' he told her. ''Certainly more quiet than it was in September of 1862.'' Because tourists inevitably enjoyed it, Devin grinned. ''You're standing right about on the spot where a Confederate soldier was killed.''

''Oh, my goodness!'' Mrs. Cox clapped her hands together. ''Did you hear that, Irma?''

''Nothing wrong with my ears, Marge.'' Mrs. Berman peered down at the stairs, as if inspecting for blood. ''Mrs. Dolin was telling us something of the history. We decided to visit the inn because we read one of the brochures that claimed it was haunted.''

''Yes, ma'am. It surely is.''

''Sheriff MacKade's brother owns the inn,'' Cassie explained. ''He can tell you quite a bit about it.''

''You can't do better than to hear it from Mrs. Dolin,'' Devin corrected. ''She lives with the ghosts every day. Tell them about the two corporals, Cassie.''

Though she told the story several times each week, Cassie had to struggle not to feel self-conscious in front of Devin. She folded her hands over her apron.

''Two young soldiers,'' she began, ''became separated from their regiments during the Battle of Antietam. Each wandered into the woods beyond the inn.

Some say they were looking for their way back to the battle, others say they were just trying to go home. Still, legend holds that they met there, fought there, each of them young, frightened, lost. They would have heard the battle still raging in the fields, over the hills, but this was one on one, strangers and enemies because one wore blue, and the other gray."

"Poor boys," Mrs. Berman murmured.

"They wounded each other, badly, and crawled off in different directions. One, the Confederate, made his way here, to this house. It's said he thought he was coming home, because all he wanted, in the end, was his home and his family. One of the servants found him, and brought him into the house. The mistress here was a Southern woman. Her name was Abigail, Abigail O'Brian Barlow. She had married a wealthy Yankee. A man she didn't love, but was bound to by her vows."

Devin's brow lifted. It was a new twist, a new detail, to the legend he had known since childhood.

"She saw the boy, a reminder of her own home and her own youth. Her heart went out to him for that, and simply because he was hurt. She ordered him to be taken upstairs, where his wounds would be tended. She spoke to him, reassured him, held his hand in hers as the servant carried him up these stairs. She knew that she could never go home again, but she wanted to be sure the boy could. The war had shown her cruelty, useless struggle and the terrible pain of loss, as her marriage had. If she could do this one thing, she thought, help this one boy, she could bear it."

Mrs. Cox took out tissues, handed one to her sister and blew her own nose hard.

"But her husband came to the stairs," Cassie continued. "She didn't hate him then. She didn't love him, but she'd been taught to respect and obey the man she had married, and the father of her children. He had a gun, and she saw what he meant to do in his eyes. She shouted for him to stop, begged him. The boy's hand was in hers, and his eyes were on her face, and if she had had the courage, she would have thrown her body over his to protect him. To save not only him, but everything she'd already lost."

Now it was Cassie who looked down at the stairs, sighed over them. "But she didn't have the courage. Her husband fired the gun and killed him, even as she held the boy's hand. He died here, the young soldier. And so did she, in her heart. She never spoke to her husband again, but she learned how to hate. And she grieved from that day until she died, two years later. And often, very often, you can smell the roses she loved in the house, and hear her weeping."

"Oh, what a sad, sad story." Mrs. Cox wiped at her eyes. "Irma, have you ever heard such a sad story?"

Mrs. Berman sniffed. "She'd have done better to have taken the gun and shot the louse."

"Yes." Cassie smiled a little. "Maybe that's one of the reasons she still weeps." She shook off the mood of the story and led the ladies the rest of the way down the steps. "If you'd like to make yourselves at home in the parlor, I'll bring in the tea I promised you."

"That would be lovely," Mrs. Cox told her, still sniffling. "Such a beautiful house. Such lovely furniture."

"All of the furnishings come from Past Times, Mrs. MacKade's shop on Main Street in town. If you have time, you might want to go in and browse. She has beautiful things, and offers a ten-percent discount to any guest of the inn."

"Ten percent," Mrs. Berman murmured, and eyed a graceful hall rack.

"Devin, would you like to have some tea?"

It took an effort to move. He wondered if she knew that Connor got his flair for telling a story from his mother.

"I'll take a rain check on that. I have something in the car for upstairs. For your place."

"Oh."

"Ladies, nice to have met you. Enjoy your stay at the MacKade Inn, and in the town."

"What a handsome man," Mrs. Cox said, with a little pat of her hand to her heart. "My goodness. Irma, have you ever seen a more handsome young man?"

But Mrs. Berman was busy sizing up the drop-leaf table in the parlor.

By the time Cassie had settled the ladies in with their tea, her curiosity was killing her. She had chores to see to, and she scolded herself for letting them lag as she hurried around to the outside stairs.

Halfway up, she saw Devin hooking up a porch swing. "Oh." It made a lovely picture, she thought, a man standing in the sunlight, his shirtsleeves rolled up, tools at his feet, muscles working as he lifted one end of the heavy wooden seat to its chain.

"This seemed like the spot for it."

"Yes, it's perfect. Rafe didn't mention that he wanted one."

"I wanted one," Devin told her. "Don't worry, I ran it by him." He hooked the other end and gave it a testing swing. "Works." Bending, he gathered up the tools. "Going to try it out with me?"

"I really have to—"

"Try it out with me," Devin finished, setting the tools aside in their case. "I put it up because I figured it was a good way to get you to sit with me on a summer afternoon. A good way for me to kiss you again."

"Oh."

"You said you didn't mind."

"No, I didn't. I don't." There it was again, that flutter in her chest. "Aren't you supposed to be working?"

"It's my day off. Sort of." He held out a hand, then curled his fingers around hers. "You look pretty today, Cassie."

Automatically she brushed at her apron. "I've been cleaning."

"Real pretty," he murmured, drawing her to the swing, and down.

"I should get you something cold to drink."

"You know, one of these days you're going to figure out that I don't come around so you can serve me cold drinks."

"Connor said you worried about me. You don't have to. I was hoping you'd come by so I could tell you how much I appreciate what you did for him the other day. The way you made him feel."

"I didn't do anything. He earned what he felt. You've got a fine boy in Connor."

"I know." She took a deep breath and relaxed enough to lean back against the seat. The rhythm of the swing took her back, far back, to childhood and sweet days, endless summers. Her lips curved, and then she laughed.

"What's funny?"

"It's just this, sitting here on a porch swing, like a couple of teenagers."

"Well, if you were sixteen again, this would be my next move." He lifted up his arms, stretched, then let one drape casually over her shoulders. "Subtle, huh?"

She laughed again, tilted her face toward his. "When I was sixteen, you were too bad to be subtle. Everybody knew how you snuck off to the quarry with girls and—"

The best way to stop her mouth was with his. He did so gently, savoring the quick tremor of her lips, of her body.

"Not so subtle," he said quietly. "Wanna go to the quarry?" When she stuttered, he only laughed. "Some other time. For now I'd settle for you kissing me back. Kiss me back, Cassie, like you were sixteen and didn't have a worry in the world."

With someone else, anyone else, he might have been amused by the concentration on her face. But it struck his heart, the way her mouth lifted to his, that hesitant pressure, the unschooled way her hands lifted to rest on his shoulders.

"Relax," he said against her mouth. "Turn off your head for a minute. Can you do that?"

"I don't..." She didn't turn it off. It shut off when his tongue danced lightly over hers, when his hands skimmed down her sides and up again. Down and up, in firm, steady strokes that had the heels of his hands just brushing the sides of her breasts.

"I love the taste of you." He pressed his lips to her jaw, her temples, back to her lips. "I've dreamed of it."

"You have?"

"Most of my life. I've wanted to be with you like this for years. Forever."

The words were seeping through that lovely haze of pleasure that covered her whenever he kissed her. "But—"

"You got married." He trailed his lips down her cheek. "I didn't move fast enough. I got drunk the day you married Joe Dolin. Blind, falling-down drunk. I didn't know what else to do. I thought about killing him, but I figured you must have wanted him. So that was that."

"Devin, I don't understand this." If he'd stop kissing her, just for a minute, she might be able to understand.

But he couldn't seem to stop, any of it. "I loved you so much I thought I'd die from it. Just keel right over and die."

Panic and denial had her struggling away. "You couldn't have."

He'd said too much, but the regrets would have to come later. Now, he'd finish it. "I've loved you for over twelve years, Cassandra. I loved you when you were married to another man, when you had his children. I loved you when I couldn't do anything to help you out of that hell you were living in. I love you now."

She got up and, in an old defensive habit, wrapped her arms tight around her body. "That's not possible."

"Don't tell me what I feel." She jolted back a full step at the anger in his tone, making him clench his teeth as he rose. "And don't you cringe away from me when I raise my voice. I can't be what I'm not, not even for you. But I'm not Joe Dolin. I'll never hit you."

"I know that." She let her arms drop. "I know that, Devin." Even as she said it, she watched him struggle to push back the worst of his temper. "I don't want you to be angry with me, Devin, but I don't know what to say to you."

"Seems like I've already said more than enough." He began to pace, his hands jammed in his pockets. "I'm good at taking things slow, thinking them through. But not this time. I've said what I've said, Cass, and I can't—won't—take it back. You're going to have to decide what you want to do about it."

"Do about what?" Baffled, she lifted her hands, then let them fall. "You want me to believe that a man like you had feelings for me all these years and didn't do anything about it?"

"What the hell was I supposed to do?" he tossed back. "You were married. You'd made your choice, and it wasn't me."

"I didn't know there was a choice."

"My mistake," he said, bitterly. "Now I've made another one, because you're not ready, or you don't want to be ready. Or maybe you just don't want me."

"I don't—" She lifted her hands to her cheeks. She honestly didn't know which, if any, of those alternatives was true. "I can't think. You've been my friend. You've been, well, the sheriff, and I've been so grateful—"

"Don't you dare say that to me." Devin shouted the words, and was too twisted with pain and fury to notice that she went white as death. "Damn it, I don't want you to be grateful. I'm not playing public servant with you. I don't deserve that."

"I didn't mean . . . Devin, I'm sorry. I'm so sorry."

"The hell with being sorry," he raged. "The hell with gratitude. You want to be grateful I locked the son of a bitch up who was pounding on you, then be grateful to the badge, not to me. Because *I* wanted to break him in half. You want to be grateful I've been coming around here being the nice guy, like some love-whipped mongrel dog, don't. Because what I've wanted to do is—"

He bit that back, his eyes cutting through her like hot knives. "You don't want to know. No, what you want is for me to keep my voice down, my feelings inside and my hands to myself."

"No, that's not—"

"You don't mind if I kiss you, but then, you're so damn grateful it's the least you can do."

Her stumbling protest fell apart. "That's not fair."

"I'm tired of being fair. I'm tired of waiting for you. I'm tired of being torn up in love with you. The hell with it."

He strode by her, and was halfway down the stairs before her legs unfroze. She raced after him. "Devin. Devin, please don't go this way. Let me—"

He jerked away from her light touch on his shoulder, whirled on her. "Leave me alone now, Cass. You want to leave me be now."

She knew that look, though she had never expected to see it aimed from his eyes into hers. It was a man's bitter fury. She had reason to fear it. Her stomach clenched painfully, but she made herself stand her ground. He would never know how much it cost her.

"You never told me," she said, fighting to keep her voice slow and even. "You never let me see. Now you have, and you won't give me time to think, to know what to do. You don't want to hear that I'm sorry, that I'm grateful, that I'm afraid. But I'm all of those things, and I can't help it. I can't make myself into what anyone else expects me to be ever again. I'll lose everything this time. If I could do it for anyone, I'd do it for you. But I can't."

"That's clear enough." He knew he was wrong—not completely wrong, but wrong enough. It just didn't seem to matter, compared with this ragged, tearing hurt inside of him. "The thing you've got twisted around, Cass, is that I don't want you to be anything but what you are. Once you figure that out, you know where to find me."

She opened her mouth again, then closed it when he strode away. There was nothing else she could say to him now, nothing else she could do. She felt raw inside, and her throat hurt.

And it was hurt that had been in his eyes, she thought, closing her own. Hurt that she had caused, without ever meaning to.

Devin MacKade loved her. The idea left her weak with terror and confusion. But bigger even than that was the idea that he had loved her all this time. Devin MacKade, the kindest, most admirable man she knew, loved her, had loved her for years, and all she had to give in return was gratitude.

Now she had lost him, the friendship she'd come to cherish, the companionship she had grown to depend on. She'd lost it because he wanted a woman, and she was empty inside.

She didn't weep. It was too late for tears. Instead, she rose, reminded herself to square her shoulders. She went back into the inn through the kitchen. There were chores to see to, and she could always think more clearly when she was working.

Her latest guests had gone off, eager to hunt antiques, so Cassie went back upstairs and turned on the vacuum she'd abandoned when the guests arrived.

She worked methodically, down the hallway, room by room. The bridal suite—Abigail's room—was her favorite. But she paid little attention now to the lovely wallpaper with its rosebuds, the graceful canopy bed, the wash of sunlight through the lace curtains.

She reminded herself to bring up fresh flowers. Even when the room wasn't occupied, there were always flowers on the table by the window. She'd forgotten them that morning.

Yet the room smelled of roses, powerfully. A sudden chill had her shivering. She felt him, and turned toward the door.

"Devin." Relief, confusion, sorrow. She experienced them all as she took a step toward the doorway.

But it wasn't Devin. The man was tall, dark-haired and handsome. But the face wasn't Devin's, and the clothes were formal, old-fashioned. Her hand went limp on the handle of the vacuum, and the sound of it buzzed in her ears.

Abigail, come with me. Take the children and come with me. Leave this place. You don't love him.

No, Cassie thought, I've never loved him. Now I despise him.

Can't you see what this is doing to you? How long will you stay, closed away from life this way?

It's all I can do. It's the best I can do.

I love you, Abby. I love you so much. I could make you happy if you'd only let me. We'll go away from here, away from him. Start our lives over, together. I've already waited for you so long.

How can I? I'm bound to him. I have the children. And you, your life is here. You can't walk away from the town, your responsibilities, the people who depend on you. You can't settle for another man's wife, another man's children.

There's nothing I wouldn't do for you. I'd kill for you. Die for you. For God's sake, Abigail, give me the

*chance to love you. All these years I've stood by,
knowing how unhappy you were, knowing you were
out of reach. That's over now. He's gone. We can leave
and be miles from here before he comes back. Why
should either of us settle for less than everything? I
don't want to sit in the parlor with you and pretend I
don't love you, don't need you. I can't keep being only
your friend.*

You know I value you, depend on you.

Tell me you love me.

I can't. I can't tell you that. There's nothing inside
me any longer. He killed it.

Come with me. And live again.

Whatever was there, whoever was there, faded, until there was only the doorway, the lovely wallpaper
and the strong, sad scent of roses. Cassie found herself standing, almost swaying, with one hand reaching out to nothing at all.

The vacuum was still humming as she sank weakly
to the floor.

What had happened here? she asked herself. Had
she been dreaming? Hallucinating?

She laid a hand on her heart and found it was beating like a wild bird in a cage. Carefully she let her head
drop down to her updrawn knees.

She had heard the ghosts before, felt them. Now,
she realized, she had seen one. Not one of the Bar-
lows, not the poor doomed soldier. But the man Abigail had loved. The man who had loved her.

Who had he been? She thought she might never
know. But his face had been compelling, though filled
with sorrow, his voice strong, even when it was plead-

ing. Why hadn't Abigail gone with him? Why hadn't she taken that hand he reached out to her and run, run for her life?

Abigail had loved him. Cassie drew in a deep breath. Of that she was sure. The emotions that swirled through the room had been so powerful, she felt them still. There had been love here. Desperate, helpless love.

Is that why you weep? Cassie wondered. Because you didn't go, and you lost him? You didn't reach out, and then there was nothing to hold on to?

You were afraid to love him, so you broke his heart.

Just as she had broken Devin's heart today.

With a shudder, Cassie lifted her head. Why? she asked herself. Out of fear and doubt. Out of habit. That was pathetic. All Devin had wanted was affection. But she hadn't told him that she cared. Hadn't showed him she cared.

Would she close herself away, as Abigail had, or would she take the chance?

Hadn't she been a coward long enough?

Wiping her damp face, she got to her feet. She had to go to him. She would go to him. Somehow.

Of course, such things are never simple. She had children, and could hardly leave them to fend for themselves. She had guests at the inn, and a job to do. It took her hours to manage it, and with every minute that passed, the doubts weighed more heavily.

She combated them by reminding herself that it didn't matter how clumsy she was. He wanted her. That would be enough.

"I'm so grateful, Ed. I know it's a lot to ask."

"Hey—" Already settled down in front of the television with a bowl of popcorn, Ed waved a hand "—so I closed a little early. I get a night off."

"The kids are asleep." But still Cassie fretted. "They hardly ever wake up after they're down."

"Don't you worry about those angels. And don't worry about the people downstairs," she added, anticipating Cassie. "They want anything, they'll call up here and let me know. I'm going to watch this love story I rented, then hit the sack."

"You take the bed. You promised," Cassie insisted. "I'll just flop down on the couch when I get back."

"Mm-hmm . . ." Ed was betting that wouldn't be until dawn. "You say hi to Devin for me, now."

Cassie twisted the collar of her blouse in her fingers. "I'm just going over to his office for a little while."

"If you say so, honey."

"He's angry with me, Ed. He's so angry with me, he might just boot me out."

Ed stopped the videotape she was watching, turned around on the couch and gave Cassie one long, summing-up look. "Honey, you look at him like that, and he's not going to boot you anywhere but into that cot he's got in the back room." When Cassie wrapped her arms around her body, Ed only laughed. "Oh, you stop that now. Devin's not going to push you into anything. A man like that doesn't have to push. He just has to be."

"How did you know I was going over there to... to try to..."

"Cassie, honey, look who you're talking to here. I've been around this block plenty. You call me, ask if I'd settle in here for the night because you need to see Devin, I'm going to figure it out. And it's long past time, if you ask me."

Cassie looked down at her plain cotton blouse and simple trousers. Her neat flat-heeled shoes. Hardly the garb of a femme fatale. "Ed, I'm no good at this sort of thing."

Ed cocked her head. "I'd wager Devin's plenty good at it, so don't you worry."

"Regan said I should let him set the pace. Maybe I shouldn't be going over there."

"Sweetie pie, sometimes even a real man needs a little kick. Now you stop second-guessing yourself and wringing your hands. Go on over there and get him."

"I should do something with my hair," Cassie fretted. "And I've chewed off my lipstick, haven't I? Maybe I should put on a dress."

"Cassie." Ed tipped down her rhinestone glasses, peered over them. "You look fine. You look fresh. He doesn't care what you're wearing, take my word for it. He's only going to care that you're there. Now go get him."

"All right." Cassie squared her shoulders, picked up her purse. "I'm going. I'm going now. But if you need anything, just—"

"I won't need a thing. Go."

"I'm going."

Ed wiggled her bright red brows as Cassie went out the door. Poor kid, she thought. She looked like she was walking out in front of a firing squad. With a cackle, Ed tipped her glasses back up and flipped the video back on.

Her money was on Devin MacKade.

Chapter 7

He really should just give it up and go back and crawl into his cot. That was what Devin told himself, but he kept right on sitting at his desk with his nose in a book. The story just wasn't holding his interest. It wasn't the fault of the author; nothing could have held his interest just then.

He knew it was foolish, and useless, but he'd had nothing and no one to vent his temper on. So there it was, still curdling inside him. He'd actually considered heading out to the farm and picking a fight with Shane. It would have been easy. Too easy. So he'd decided against it.

He told himself it was because he was a better man than that. He'd have done that sort of thing in his teens—hell, in his twenties. The fact was, he'd probably have done it last week.

But it just didn't suit his mood now.

He was just going to sit here, in his quiet office, with his feet up on his desk and the chair kicked back, and read. Even if it killed him.

It was after ten on a weeknight, which meant it was doubtful any calls were going to come in to liven things up. He didn't have to be there, but he liked the solitude of his office at night, the familiarity of it. And the fact that he could be there, behind the desk instead of behind the bars.

He hadn't even turned the radio on, as he often did to bring a little music and company into the night. The only light was the one on his desk, the metal gooseneck lamp aimed at the book in his hands. The book he wasn't reading.

He considered getting up and brewing coffee, since he wasn't going to bed. But it seemed like too much effort.

It was the first time in his life he could remember being so angry and so tired at the same time. Usually temper energized him, got his blood up and his adrenaline sizzling. Now he was sapped. He supposed it was because most of the anger was self-directed, though he still had plenty left over for Cassie.

When a woman hurt a man, it was the most natural thing in the world to cover it with anger.

He'd told other women he loved them. He wouldn't have denied it. The fact was that he'd tried to love other women. He'd worked hard at it for a space of time. The last thing he'd wanted to do was moon around over something he couldn't have.

Which was just what he was doing now.

Sulking, his mother would have called it, he thought with a grimace. He missed her more just now than he had since she'd died. And he'd missed her quite a bit over the years.

She'd have given him a cuff on the ear, he supposed, or she'd have laughed. She'd have told him to get his sorry butt up and do something instead of brooding over what he should have done. Or shouldn't have done.

Well, he couldn't think of anything to do, except count his losses. He'd moved too quick, pushed too hard, and he'd stumbled over his own heart.

The hell with it, Devin thought again, and let the book lie on his chest. Shifting in the chair, he closed his eyes and ordered himself to think about something else.

He needed to talk to the mayor about getting a stop sign out on the end of Reno Road. Three serious accidents there in a year was reason enough to push for it. Then there was the talk he'd promised to give at the high school for the last assembly before summer hit. And he really had to help Shane with the early haying . . .

The dream snuck up on him, sly and crafty. Somehow he'd gotten from the hayfield to her bedroom door. Cassie? No, that wasn't Cassie. Abigail. Love and longing stirred in him. Why couldn't she see that she needed him as much as he needed her? Would she just sit there with her hands folded in her lap over her embroidery, her eyes tired and lost?

It seemed nothing he could say would convince her to come with him, to let him love her, as surely he'd been born to do. No, she would close herself off from him, from everything they could have. Should have.

Anger stirred along with the love, along with the longing. He was tired of coming begging, with his hat in his hand.

I won't ask again, he told her, and she just watched him. *I won't come to you again and have you break my heart. I've waited long enough. If this is the way it has to be, I'm leaving Antietam. I can't keep running the law here, knowing you're here, always out of reach. I have to pick up whatever pieces are left of my life and go.*

But she said nothing, and he knew when he stepped back, walked down the hall and down the stairs that it was the end. Her weeping drifted to him when he left the house.

Cassie stood on the other side of the desk, twisting the strap of her purse in her fingers. She hadn't expected to find him asleep, didn't know if she would wake him or leave as quietly as she had come.

There was nothing peaceful about him. There should have been, the way his feet were propped on the desk, crossed at the ankles, the way the book was lying open against his chest, the desk lamp slanting light over it.

But his face was hard and tense, his mouth grim. She wished she had the courage to smooth those lines away and make him smile.

Then again, courage had always been her problem.

He opened his eyes and had her jumping like a rabbit. "I'm sorry. I didn't mean to wake you."

"I wasn't asleep." At least he didn't think he'd been asleep. His brain was fuzzy and full of the scent of roses, and for a moment he'd thought she was wearing some full-skirted blue gown, with lace at the throat.

Of course, she wasn't. Just her tidy little blouse and slacks, he thought, dragging a hand through his hair. "I was just going over some things in my head. Town business."

"If you're busy, I can—"

"What do you want, Cassie?"

"I . . ." He was still angry. She had expected that, was prepared for it. "I have some things to say to you."

"All right. Go ahead."

"I know I hurt you, and that you're furious with me. You don't want me to apologize. You get mad when I do, so I won't."

"Fine. Aren't you going to make me coffee?"

"Oh, I—" She'd already turned to the pot before she caught herself. She drew a breath, turned back and faced him. He had a brow lifted. "No."

"Well, that's something."

"I'm used to waiting on people." Now she was irritated, a not entirely unpleasant sensation, even if an unfamiliar one. "If it annoys you, I can't help it. Maybe I like waiting on people. Maybe it makes me feel useful."

"I don't want you to wait on me." He could see the irritation clearly enough. It added a snap to her eyes that fascinated him. "I don't want you to feel obliged to me."

"Well, I do feel obliged. And I can't help that, either. And the fact that I do feel obliged and do feel grateful— Don't shout at me, Devin."

Impressed with her no-nonsense tone, he closed his mouth, then added, "I might yet."

"At least wait until I've finished." It wasn't so hard, she realized. It was like dealing with the children, really. You just had to be fair and firm, and not allow yourself to be sidetracked. "I have good reasons to feel obliged to you, and grateful to you, but that doesn't meant that beyond that, or besides that... It doesn't mean I don't have other feelings, too."

"Such as?"

"I don't know, exactly. I haven't had real feelings for a man in—maybe never," she decided. "But I don't want to lose your friendship and... affection. Next to the children, there's no one I care for more than you, Devin. Being with you..." She was going to fumble now, and she hated herself for it. "The way we were today, this afternoon, before you got mad, was so nice, it was so special."

She was cutting right through his temper, slicing it to ribbons, the way she was standing there, twisting her purse strap and struggling to find a way to put things right between them.

"Okay, Cassie, why don't we—"

"I came here to go to bed with you."

His jaw dropped. He was sure he heard it hit the edge of the desk. Before he could pick it up again, the door burst open and Shane strolled in.

"Hey, Dev. Hey there, Cassie. Thought you might want to go down to Duff's and shoot a couple games.

Why don't you come along, Cassie? It's about time you learned how to shoot pool."

"Go away, Shane," Devin muttered, without taking his eyes off Cassie's face.

"Come on, Dev, you've got nothing to do around here except read another book and drink stale coffee." Experimentally he picked up the pot and sniffed. "This stuff'll kill you."

"Get lost now, or die."

"What's the problem? We'll just—" All innocence, Shane turned back. The tension in the air struck him like a fist, the way his brother was staring at Cassie. The way she was staring back. "Oh. Oh," he repeated, drawing out the word on a milewide grin. "Well, son of a gun. Who'd have thought?"

"You've got ten seconds to get out the door before I shoot you."

"Well, hell, I'm going. How was I supposed to know you and Cassie were—"

"Tomorrow," Devin said evenly, and finally managed to get his feet off the desk and onto the floor, "I'm going to break you into very small pieces."

"Yeah, right. I guess you two don't want to play pool, so I'll be going. Ah, want me to lock this?" he said, winking as Devin snarled at him. But he was obliging enough to flip the latch and shut the door snugly behind him.

"You're not really going to fight with him?" Cassie began quickly. "He didn't mean anything, and..." Tongue-tied, she let her words trail off as Devin walked slowly around the desk.

"What did you say to me before my idiot brother came in?"

"That I came here to go to bed with you."

"That's what I thought you said. Is this your way of mending fences and keeping my friendship? Some new way of apologizing?"

"No." Oh, she was making a mess of it. He didn't look amorous, just curious. "Yes, maybe. I'm not sure. I know, at least, I thought you wanted to. Don't you?"

"I'm asking what you want."

"I'm telling you." Lord, hadn't she just said it, out loud, in plain words? "I came here, didn't I? I called Ed, and she's staying with the kids, and I'm here." She shut her eyes briefly. "It isn't easy for me, Devin."

"I can see that. Cassie, I want you, but what I don't want is for you to think this is necessary to make things up with me."

She did what she had done once before. It had worked then. Cupping her hand on his cheek, she leaned up and kissed him.

"Now you're waiting for me to jump you," Devin murmured.

"Oh, I'm no good at this." In disgust, she tossed her purse into a chair. "I never have been."

"At sex?"

"Of course at sex. What else are we talking about?"

"I wonder," he said quietly, but she was off and running in a way he'd never seen or heard before.

"I don't know what you want, or how to give it. If you'd just do whatever you usually do, it would be all right. It's not that I won't like it, I will. I'm sure I will.

It's not your fault that I'm clumsy or stiff, or that I don't have orgasms."

She broke off in horror, and saw that he was gaping at her.

"Excuse me?"

Someone else had said that, she thought frantically, looking everywhere but at him. Surely someone else had said that. All she could do to cover the overwhelming tide of horrid embarrassment was to rush on.

"What I mean is, I want to go to bed with you. I know it'll be nice, because it's nice when you kiss me, so I'm sure the rest will be, too. And if you'd just *do* something, I wouldn't be feeling so stupid."

What the hell was he supposed to do? He knew very well the woman standing there was the mother of two, had been married for a decade. And he'd just realized she was as close to a virgin as anyone he'd ever touched.

It scared the living hell out of him.

He started to tell her that they would take a step back, take it slow. Then he knew that was the wrong way to go. It was painfully obvious that so much of her had been crushed already. What he would know was patience, she would see as rejection.

"I should do what I want with you?"

Enormously relieved, she smiled. "Yes."

It was an offer that had the juices flowing hot. He knew if he wanted this to work he had to clamp down on needs—and on nerves. "And I'll tell you what to do, and you'll do it."

"Yes." Oh, it was really so simple. "If you just don't expect too much, and you—"

"Why don't we start this way?" He put his hands on her shoulders and lowered his mouth gently to hers. "There's something I want very much, Cassie."

"All right."

"I want you to say you're not afraid of me, that you know I won't hurt you."

"I'm not. I know you won't."

"And I want you to promise something." He skimmed his lips up her jaw, felt her shoulders relax under his hands.

"All right."

"That you'll say stop if you mean stop, if I do something you don't like."

"You won't."

His lips cruised around to her ear and made something quake inside her. "Promise me."

"I promise."

He took her hand and led her through the door into the small room he used at night. It was dark. It held little more than a narrow bed, a rickety table, an ashtray he rarely used anymore.

"It shouldn't be here. I should take you somewhere."

"No." If it wasn't now, she'd lose her nerve. What difference did atmosphere make, when it was dark and her eyes were closed? "This is fine."

"We'll make it better than fine."

He lit one of the station's emergency candles, so at least there was soft light. She couldn't know how arousing she was, standing there, tidy and terrified, prepared to give herself. To sacrifice herself, he thought grimly.

He would show her different.

"I love you, Cassie." It didn't matter that she didn't believe him. She would. He kissed her again, slowly, deeply, patiently, putting his heart into it.

And moment after moment there was nothing but the kiss, the taste of it, the meeting of lips, the way she softened against him.

"Hold me," he murmured.

Obedient, wanting to please, she wrapped her arms around him. There was a little shock when she felt how hard he was, how strong. How odd it was to hold him tight against her. While his mouth moved over hers, she stroked her hands over his back.

"I want to see you." He continued to rub his lips over her throat, even as her hands tensed on his back. He didn't mind her being shy. He found it endearing. "You have such a lovely face." His eyes stayed on it as he slowly undid the buttons of her blouse. "Eyes like fog, and that sexy mouth."

She blinked, thrown off enough to make no protest when he parted her blouse. No one had ever called her sexy. Then his gaze shifted downward, and the sound that rumbled in his throat had something curling hard in her stomach.

He was cupping her breasts in his hands, holding them as if they were delicate glass that could be shattered by a careless touch.

"Lovely."

"I'm small."

"Perfect." He lifted his gaze to hers again. "Just perfect." He watched her lashes flutter when he circled her breasts, brushed his thumbs over her nipples. And his blood heated when they stiffened, when she shuddered, when her eyes opened again in surprise and went dark.

What was he doing? Why wasn't he squeezing or pulling? She felt her head spin before it fell back. Heard, with a kind of dull shock, her own moan.

"Do you have to close your eyes?" he asked her. It wasn't so difficult to keep his hands easy, after all, not on skin that was soft as silk. "I like to watch them go cloudy when I touch you. I love to touch you, Cassie."

"I can't breathe."

"You're breathing. I can feel your heart." He lowered his lips to her shoulder before straightening to pull off his shirt. "Feel mine."

My oh my, Cassie thought. He looked like something in one of those glossy magazines. All muscles and firm smooth skin. With only the slightest of hesitations, she laid a hand on his chest, and smiled. "It's pounding. Are you ready?"

"Oh, Cassie." Biting back a groan, he drew her into his arms, cradled her there, savored the feel of her flesh pressed against his. "I haven't even started."

Because she thought he meant something entirely different, her brows drew together and she swallowed her distaste and reached courageously for his crotch.

With a ripe oath, he jerked back, stuttering, as she covered herself and gaped.

"I thought you wanted... I thought you meant..."
Good God, he'd been hard as rock. And huge.

He decided laughing would be better than scream-ing. "Darlin', you do that again, I'm going to embar-rass myself, and we'll have to start all over. If it's all the same to you, I'd just like to touch you for a while."

"I don't mind, but you're..."

"I know what I am. You said you'd do what I want," he reminded her, fighting to keep his voice from growing rough with need. "I want you to look at me, look right at me now."

When she did, he skimmed his hands over her breasts again. He could see surprised pleasure ripple over her face, hear it in her quickening breaths. So he began to murmur to her, endearments, foolishness, gauging her reaction.

When her eyes closed, he lifted her slowly off her feet, holding her suspended, trailing his mouth down from hers and over her throat, her collarbone, and at last to her breast.

Her hands clamped on his shoulders and her body arched as arrows—bullets—of hot sensation pierced through her flesh and straight to her center to burn. She shook her head, struggling to clear it.

"Devin."

He laved his tongue over her. "Do you want me to stop?"

"No. No."

"Thank God."

When she was quivering, when her hands were clutching and flexing on his skin, he lowered her to the floor again, until his mouth was fixed on hers. Her

hands were fisted in his hair, her breath was coming
fast. Her lips were hot.

And still she stiffened, just for an instant, when he
unhooked her slacks.

She wouldn't spoil it. That she promised herself.
Whatever came now didn't matter, because what came
before had been so lovely. She'd never felt these pulls,
these yearnings. Or she'd somehow forgotten them.
His hands were hard, the palms rough, but he used
them so gently on her. She would have been happy to
have him go on touching her, just like this, forever.
She could blissfully have drowned in those wonderful
ripples of sensations.

Now he was uncovering the rest of her, and she
knew it would be over soon. But he would hold her
when he was done. He would hold her close and
warm, she was sure of it. That would be enough.

When he picked her up and cradled her against his
chest, she smiled. The candlelight was lovely, and she
felt an intense sense of tenderness, of sweetness. He'd
made her feel wanted. She laid her lips against his,
curled her arms around his neck, keeping them there
as he lowered her to the cot so that the springs
squeaked under their weight.

She opened her eyes in confusion when he didn't
push inside her. Instead, he was curved beside her, his
eyes on her face, his hand stroking up and down her
torso.

"Don't rush me," he said mildly. "I'm enjoying
myself."

To her astonishment, he began to talk to her about her body, her skin, her eyes, her legs. And the things he was murmuring sent flashes of new heat inside her.

She was grateful he didn't seem to need her to talk back. She was having trouble breathing again.

She was so incredibly sweet, so amazingly innocent. That was what kept his need locked away, kept his hands from taking quickly. Twelve years, he thought, listening to the way her breath caught, then burst out, when he skimmed a finger up the inside of her thigh. When a man had waited so long, he could be as patient as a saint, though his blood churned like a riptide.

He lowered his mouth to her breast again. So small, and firm, and smelling like spring. Under his lips he felt her heart thundering, felt her skin quiver. And knew he pleasured her.

He wanted to give her more, to give her everything, to know she craved as he did. So he stroked and suckled, arousing himself and her until she began to writhe under him and he knew she was climbing toward the edge. And he would be the one to show her that the fall was sweet.

It was too hot. She was burning from the inside out and couldn't keep still. She ached, and nothing she could do seemed to soothe the throbbing. Something inside her was racing for something else, and she strained away from it. It was too big, too huge, too terrifying. The air was thick, the sensations were too fast and too many. She moaned and bit down on her lip to stop the sound.

"You can yell," Devin told her, his own voice ragged. "You can scream if you want. Nobody can hear but me. Just let go, Cassie."

"I can't."

He dipped his fingers inside her, and his head spun. She was hot and wet and more ready than she knew. "Don't ask me to stop," he murmured against her mouth. "Don't ask me."

"No. No, don't."

She did scream then, a sound that should have shocked her, it was so wild and wanton. But her body was too busy rearing up toward him, poised on a spear of dark, drenching pleasure such as she'd never known. Everything inside her came to a fist, tensed violently, painfully, then burst free. She collapsed, weak as water, and thought she heard him groan.

"Again." He was greedy now. He kept a hand fisted in the tousled sheet to keep himself sane, and urged her up, urged her over. She strained against his hand, poured into it, and the arms she'd wrapped around him slid bonelessly to the mattress.

Surrender, he thought. More, fulfillment. But now he would give her himself.

He covered her, slipped inside her, holding himself back as her eyes fluttered open on fresh shock. He took her slowly, drawing out each stroke, each pulse. His heart almost burst from the strain of control when she convulsed again. Deliberately, patiently, he stirred her, gaining unimagined joy as he felt her begin once more to tremble and race.

The shudder worked through him, ripping, demanding. This time he knew he would go with her.

Finally, with her. He clenched at the hand she'd fisted in the sheet, covered it. And took the fall.

She couldn't stop shuddering. But she wasn't cold. Not cold at all. The heat from her body, and from Devin's, which lay over her, seemed to rise in waves that were all but visible. He was breathing hard, like a man who'd been racing, and his full weight was on her, pinning her to the mattress so that she could feel the springs pushing against her back.

It was lovely.

She understood, for the first time in her life, the secrets of the dark.

"I know I'm crushing you," he managed. "I'm trying to move."

"You can stay." She wrapped her arms around him to keep him there. He was still inside her, still there. It felt wicked and wonderful. "I like it this way."

"I appreciate you putting up with all that, seeing as you're not big on sex."

The dry tone alerted her, but she was too delighted to mind being teased. "I didn't mind," she said, and smiled against his throat. "Devin, it was wonderful. I actually—"

"I know. Several times. I counted."

She laughed, and didn't feel at all embarrassed. "You did not."

"I certainly did." He found the energy to lift his head and look down at her. "You can thank me later."

Her smile sweetened. She'd never had a man look at her like that, all hazy-eyed and satisfied and sleepy. "It was all right." Incredibly moved, she lifted a hand to his cheek. "Wasn't it?"

"It was worth waiting for." He turned his lips into her palm. "But I'm not waiting another twelve years to have you again."

"I don't want you to." Everything inside her was dreamy and disjointed. "You're so handsome."

"The curse of the MacKades."

"I mean it." She lifted her other hand, framing his face. It was so easy to touch him now, to let her finger trace that wonderful dimple beside his smile. "Do you remember how I used to come out to the farm sometimes when I was a girl, to visit with your mother?"

"Sure. You were a pretty little thing, skinny, and I didn't pay you much mind. My mistake."

"I used to watch you. In the summer, especially. When you'd be working with your shirt off."

His grin flashed. "Well, well, little Cassie..."

"I had a terrible crush on you for a while, and these really imaginative fantasies." She chuckled. "Well, I thought they were imaginative, until now. Nothing came close. I can't believe I'm saying this, talking to you like this."

"Under the circumstances, you can say pretty much anything." He was hoping she would. He could feel himself hardening inside her.

"I was about twelve, and you were always nice to me. All of you were. I loved coming out there, just to be there. But it was a bonus when it was summer and you'd be bare-chested and sweaty. Like you are now."

Experimentally, she traced a finger over his shoulder. "All those muscles shiny with damp. Your body...it's so beautiful. Sometimes you'd come into Ed's, and when you'd go out, if there were women in there, they'd roll their eyes and sigh."

"Come on."

"Really. Of course, if one of your brothers came in, they'd do the same thing."

"Don't spoil it."

She laughed, lifting a hand to push tousled hair from her cheek. "Okay. They sighed louder, and longer, for you."

"That's better."

"And Ed would say something like 'That Devin MacKade's got the best buns in three counties.'" She caught herself on a giggle, her eyes going wide. "I shouldn't have said that."

"Too late. Besides, I know Ed's partial to that particular part of the anatomy. She's told me."

"She's shameless." With a long sigh of her own, Cassie wound her arms around him again, let her hands wander down. "But you do have an exceptional seat."

"Now you've done it." As her fingers brushed over his hips, he began to move inside her. Nothing could have pleased him more than seeing the way her eyes rounded in surprise.

"But how can you— Oh my God!"

"It's no trouble," he assured her. "It's my pleasure."

And after, a long time after, he curled up beside her on the cot, his face buried in her hair, his legs tangled with hers. As she had hoped, as she had needed, he held her.

Chapter 8

It was barely dawn when Cassie crept into her own kitchen. She felt giddy, like a teenager sneaking home after curfew. Not that she'd ever broken curfew, she thought now. Not that she'd ever done anything except exactly what was expected of her.

It made her hushed, secret return all the more liberating.

She'd just spent the night, all night, with the most exciting, beautiful, the most gentle man she'd ever known.

She, Cassandra Connor Dolin, was having an affair.

She had to slap her hand over her mouth to muffle a burst of laughter. Her heart was still racing, her head still swimming, and her body...her body felt as though it had been polished with flower petals.

She was sure she looked different, and tried to see her reflection in the chrome of the toaster. Because she was alone, she allowed herself three quick spins before putting the kettle on for coffee.

Then, being a mother, she padded toward the bedrooms to make sure her children were snug and asleep. Turning from Connor's room, she stifled a gasp. There was Ed, her fire-engine hair done up in squashy pink rollers, wearing a wildly flowered robe of pink and blue.

"I'm sorry," Cassie whispered. "I didn't mean to wake you."

"You were quiet as a little mouse. I was listening out for you." Ed took a long, measuring look, and liked what she saw. "Well, well, I believe you're feeling good and smug this morning. About time, too."

Cassie cast a last look at her sleeping son, then backed down the short hallway toward the kitchen. "The kids didn't give you any trouble, did they?"

"Of course not. Never heard a peep out of either of them." Grinning, Ed followed Cassie into the kitchen, watched while she busied herself measuring out coffee. "You going to tell me about it, or am I going to have to use my imagination? I got a damn good one."

The heat rose to Cassie's cheeks, but it was from pleasure as much as embarrassment. "I stayed with Devin."

"I figured that out, sweetie pie." Very much at home, Ed popped bread into the toaster. "From the look on your face, the two of you didn't discuss world events until morning." Sighing a little, she poked around in the refrigerator. "I'm not just being nosy. I guess I want to make sure you're as okay on the inside as you look on the out."

"I'm fine." Cassie turned, smiled. There was Ed, holding a jar of preserves in one hand and a gallon of milk in the other, her thin face shiny with night cream, her hair exploding on rollers, her outrageous robe falling over legs the shape of toothpicks.

This, Cassie realized, was the mother of her heart. Cassie set the steaming kettle down again and dashed over to throw her arms around Ed.

Surprised, moved, Ed pressed her lips to Cassie's hair. "There, baby..."

"I feel ... different. Do I look different?"

"You look happy."

"My stomach's still jumping." Laughing at herself, Cassie drew back and pressed a hand to it. "But it feels good. I didn't know it could be like that. I didn't know I could be like that." Casting a quick look at the hallway, she went back to the coffee. Her children were asleep, and would be for another half hour. After all these years, Cassie thought, she would have a mother to listen.

"I've never been with anyone but Joe."

"I know that, baby."

"Before we were married, I wouldn't let him. I wanted to be married first, I wanted it to be right." She poured coffee for both of them, then sat at the table. "I was nervous on our wedding night, but excited, too. You'd given me a white nightgown for my shower. It was so pretty, so perfect. It made me feel like a bride. When we got to the motel, I asked Joe to give me an hour to myself. I wanted to take a long bath and . . . well, you know."

"The female ritual. Yeah, I know."

"He came back—it was closer to two hours—and he was drunk. It wasn't the way I'd always dreamed. He ripped the gown, and he pushed me onto the bed. It all happened so fast, and he hurt me. I knew it was supposed to hurt some the first time, but it was more than some. He fell asleep right after, and I just laid there. I didn't feel anything."

"A man's not supposed to treat a woman that way." Even if she hadn't already despised Joe Dolin, Ed would have despised him now. "That's not how it's supposed to be."

"It was the way it was. Always. I never felt anything, Ed. Ever. He didn't always hurt me, but it was always quick, and mostly a little mean. I figured it was my fault—he told me it was often enough. It got better when I was carrying Connor, because he left me alone most of the time. I didn't know he was cheating on me then. I guess I was too stupid."

"Don't you call yourself stupid," Ed said fiercely. "I don't want to hear that."

"Maybe I just didn't care enough to know, or want to know. I was wrapped up in becoming a mother, then in being one. He was already hitting me. We hadn't been married long when that started, but I didn't think there was anything I could do about it. My mother said . . . well, it doesn't matter what she said. I stayed, then Emma came along. He only wanted me a couple of times after Emma . . . He forced me."

"Oh, Cassie. Honey, why didn't you tell me?"

"Ed, I was too ashamed. He was my husband, and I had it in my head that he had a right to do what he did. I know different now." She took a long breath. "You see, when I went to Devin last night, I didn't think... I knew he wouldn't hurt me, at least not like Joe had. I thought going to bed with him would make him happy, and it didn't matter to me. I mean, I thought he would just... that I would just..."

"You had yourself a real man last night," Ed finished. "And it changed things."

"Yes." Relieved, Cassie smiled. "He was so gentle, so patient. You know, it mattered to him what I was feeling. It really mattered. And he made me feel beautiful. Ed..." She bit her lip, even as it curved again. "It matters to me now. I'm already thinking about next time."

Ed let out a cackling laugh and squeezed Cassie's hand. "Good for you."

"He says he loves me," Cassie said quietly. "I know men say those things when they want you, or they think you need to hear it. But do you think he could?"

"I think Devin MacKade's a man who says what he means. What about you?"

"I don't know. That part of me is so confused. I didn't love Joe, Ed. I never did. I used him."

"Cassandra—"

"No, I did. I used him to get out of the house, because I wanted to have a family of my own, and he was there. I wasn't fair to him. I don't mean that gave him the right to beat me," she added, noting the warrior gleam in Ed's eye. "Nothing gave him that right. But

I didn't love him, not the way a woman should love her husband."

"He didn't do anything to deserve love."

"No, he didn't. With Devin, I feel so many things, so many different things, and I don't know if one of them is that kind of love."

"Then you take all the time you need to sort it out. Don't you let anyone push you into anything you're not ready for. Not even Devin."

"How will I know?"

"Sweetie pie, when the time comes you'll know. Take my word for it, you'll know."

While Cassie was talking with Ed over coffee, Devin was pulling up at the farm. He'd felt a need for home. The sky was losing its dawn haze when he walked into the milking parlor. Shane and two of the 4-H students he often took on as help were finishing up the morning routine.

Patiently Shane showed one of the boys how to detach cow from machine without causing irritation. The parlor smelled of warm milk, animal and hay.

"You're going to check her teats after, just like you did before, to make sure there's no infection." He did so himself, demonstrating. "When she's dry, you see to her feed." He cocked a brow at Devin. "You can see the sheriff wanders in when most of the work's done. Y'all lead them out now."

Devin gave the cow an easy swat, then helped Shane clean and disinfect the machines. It was routine, companionable work.

"Remember when Dad had us milking by hand?" Devin asked.

"He figured we'd better know. Machines break down, but cows fill up regular. You're up early," Shane commented. "And you've got a stupid grin on your face. Looks like you got lucky."

Devin only angled his head. "I'm feeling too good to pound on you this morning."

"Good, because I've got to finish up here and get to the hens before breakfast. You and Cassie," he said, grinning again. "Who'd have thought it?"

"I've been thinking about it for a long time." Devin helped Shane secure the fresh milk in the stainless-steel tanks. "I've been in love with her a long time."

Shane straightened, winced. "Man, don't start that. Every time I turn around, somebody's falling in love. It's giving me nightmares."

"Well, get used to it. I'm going to ask her to marry me."

Shane rubbed his hands over his face, pulled off his cap, dragged hands through his hair. "What is it? Something in the water around here? First Rafe, then Jared. Now you. I turn my back for a minute and everybody's getting married, having babies. Get a hold of yourself, Dev."

"Afraid it's going to rub off?"

"Hell, I'm going to start to take shots. Look, Cassie's as sweet as they come, and as pretty as fresh milk, but let's not go crazy."

"I love her," Devin said, so simply Shane groaned. "It seems I always have. There's nothing I could do about it even if I wanted to."

"You know what kind of trouble this is going to cause me? Don't you have any consideration?" Shane demanded. "I'll be the only one of us left. Women home in on things like that. I won't be able to get myself a snuggle without the woman thinking it's going to lead to orange blossoms."

"You'll have to tough it out."

"What in sweet hell's so appealing about marriage?" Grumbling, Shane headed out of the milking parlor. "I mean, think about it, Dev. Really think. You've got one woman for the rest of your life. Just one. And there're so many out there. Tall ones, short ones, round ones."

Amused, Devin slapped a hand on Shane's shoulder as they walked toward the chicken coop. "And with me out of the way, there'll be more for you."

"There is that." Taking it philosophically, Shane shrugged. "I guess it'll be up to me to maintain the MacKade legend. I'll just have to make the sacrifice."

"You're up to it, bro."

Cassie never lingered in the library. She was much too conscientious to skim over her cleaning there, but most often she tried to arrange her schedule so that someone was in the house when she dealt with that room.

There was no one in the house now. Her children were in school and the guests were busy with their sight-seeing for the afternoon. She made excuses in her head for why she should see to a dozen other things besides that one room. But she knew the library had been used the day before. She knew there were books that needed to be put back on the shelves, plants that needed watering, windows that needed washing.

She told herself it was foolish. She knew the emotions and moods of the house better than she knew her own. There was nothing here that could hurt her. In fact, the house had changed her life, and all for the better.

Armed with her cleaning basket, she went in. If she left the door open wide behind her, it was only because she wanted to be able to hear if one of the guests returned and wanted anything.

It wasn't because she was afraid.

She set the basket aside and tidied the books first. She knew guests often liked to borrow one to read on a rainy afternoon or to help them drift off to sleep at night. Rafe and Regan had provided a variety of books for a variety of tastes. She, too, was free to borrow any she liked, whenever she liked. But she rarely did.

Nor, she thought suddenly, did Connor, though he was a voracious reader. It occurred to her that he, too, avoided this room, even though he was thoroughly at home in the rest of the inn.

It was a feeling, she supposed. Something that lingered in the air. Shaking it off, she carried her basket over to the twin philodendrons that trailed their leaves from pots set in stands by the tall window that overlooked the side garden.

They needed to be dusted. She'd been putting it off.

As she began, she felt the chill, down to the bone.

And knew she wasn't really alone.

She thought she could see him, out of the corner of her eye. The big body going to fat, the wide face set in hard, dissatisfied lines.

Joe.

The terror came so quickly, she dropped the basket at her feet as she whirled around.

He wasn't there. Of course he wasn't. No one was. But it was so bitterly cold. With numb fingers, she reached for the window to open it to the warm breeze.

She fumbled, couldn't work the latch, and discovered her breath was coming in short gasps.

You let him touch you, didn't you? Whore.

She hunched her shoulders automatically against a blow that didn't come.

Did you think I wouldn't know? Did you think you could cuckold me in my own house? You, with your innocent face and fancy Southern manners. Nothing but a slut.

Shaking, she backed slowly away from the window. Her eyes darted around the room, searching corners. There was no one there. But how could she hear the voice so clearly in her head?

Know this. You'll never leave me. I'll see you dead first.

You don't love me, Cassie wanted to say. You despise me. Let me go. But the words wouldn't come.

I'll kill you both. Remember that. Till death do us part. And death is your only escape.

"Cassie."

On a strangled shriek, she spun around. Devin was just inside the door, his eyes narrowed in concern. Without a thought, she ran into his arms.

"Devin. Devin, you have to go. Go quickly, before he sees you. He's going to kill you."

"What are you talking about? God, you're shaking like a leaf. It's freezing in here."

"You feel it?" Her teeth were all but chattering as she drew back. "You can feel it?"

"Sure I can. It's like an icebox." He rubbed her hands in his to warm them.

"I thought it was Joe. I swear I saw his fist coming toward me, and then—" The room spun; her knees buckled. The dizziness lasted only an instant, but she was already up in Devin's arms. "I'm all right. It's gone."

The room was warm again, sunny and bright, with the scent of roses and polish. Very gently, he laid her down on the soft leather sofa. "Let me get you some water."

"No, I'm all right." She thought she might jump out of her skin if he left her alone there. "It's just this room." She steadied herself, sat up. "I thought it was Joe, but it wasn't. It was Barlow."

She was still too pale, Devin thought, but her eyes had cleared. His heart had dropped to his knees when he'd seen them roll back in her head. "Has this happened before?"

"Not like this. Not this strong. I'm never very comfortable in this room. Even his bedroom is easier. But this time, I heard... You're going to think I've lost my mind."

"No, I won't." He cupped her face in his hands. "Remember who you're talking to."

"All right." She blew out a breath. "I heard him talking, in my head, I think. It sounded so much like Joe—the tone, the meanness in it. He called me—her—a whore, a slut. He knew she was in love with someone else, but he wasn't going to let her go, ever. He said he'd kill her first, kill both of them."

"Come on, let's get out of here. Let's go upstairs."

"I haven't finished—"

"Leave it, Cassie. Just leave it." He would have carried her, but she got to her feet. Still, her hand reached for his. "The other day, when you were talking to the old ladies?"

"Mrs. Cox and Mrs. Berman, yes."

"You talked about Abigail being in love with someone. I thought you'd made it up, to add a little romance to the story."

"No. I can't explain it, Devin. I just know it's true. I saw him."

He paused at the back stairs that led up to her apartment. "You saw who?"

"The man she loved. I was in her room, and then I looked and he was at the door. He was looking right at me, talking to me as if I were Abigail. I could feel her there. Her heart was broken, but she let him go. Made him go. Devin...Devin, I think she killed herself."

He sat her down in a chair in her living room. "Why do you think that?"

"I can't explain that, either. Just a feeling. She didn't know how else to get free. And maybe because I thought about it once."

The blood drained from his face. "Good God, Cassie."

"Not for very long," she said quickly. "And not very seriously. I had the kids to think about. If I hadn't had them, I might have thought about it longer. When you're trapped, Devin, you get crazy ideas about escape."

Nothing he knew about her had ever frightened him more. "I would have helped you. I wanted to help you."

"I wouldn't let you. I wouldn't let anyone. You, Ed, Regan. There were others, too, others who were willing to do whatever they could. I was wrong not to accept the help, but that's over now." She curled her hands over his. "I'm not telling you this to upset you, but to try to help you understand how I know she did it. She didn't have people to help her. He'd seen to that. He made sure she was cut off from the women in town, made sure the servants were too frightened to do anything but stand back."

Somewhere in her mind, she could almost feel it, see it. "He hit her, too. It was his fist I saw today. Not Joe's. But it's the same, you see. So much the same. When he killed that boy in front of her, she knew he was capable of anything. She gave up, Devin. Eventually even her children weren't enough to keep her from escaping in the only way she knew."

"It's not you, Cassie."

"It could have been."

"But it's not," he said firmly. "You're here, you're with me. There's nothing for you to be afraid of."

"I'm tired of being afraid." She closed her eyes, let her head rest on his shoulder as he crouched in front of her. "I'm glad you're here." She let out a deep sigh. "Why are you here?"

"I worked it so I could clear out for an hour. I wanted to see you. I wanted to be with you."

"I thought about you all morning. I nearly put coffee in Emma's thermos for school, because I was thinking about you instead of what I was doing."

"Really?" He couldn't think of a more satisfying compliment. When she lifted her head, he could see that the color was back in her cheeks. "Were you thinking that you'd like to make love with me again?"

"Yes, I was."

"I've still got most of an hour," he murmured, rising and bringing her to her feet.

She blinked. "It's the middle of the day."

"Uh-huh." He drew her toward the hall.

"Devin, it's daylight."

"That's right." He unhooked his belt that held his beeper and weapon, hung them over the doorknob.

"It's . . ." Her heart stumbled as he reached out to unbutton her blouse. "It's barely noon."

"Yeah, I'm going to miss lunch." As he slipped the blouse from her shoulders, lowered his mouth toward hers, he smiled. "Do you want me to stop, Cassie?"

Her head rolled back on her shoulders. "I guess I don't," she said, weak, willing.

She forgot that the sun was shining and the birds were twittering. She forgot that traffic was cruising by on the road, and that people were going about their business in town.

It was so easy, so powerfully easy, to let it all happen again. It was so easy to enjoy the way his hands moved tenderly over her, the way his mouth coaxed hers to warm. He felt so good against her when she curled her arms around him, so solid, that she forgot to feel self-conscious because the sun was pouring through the windows.

He undressed her, completely, taking his time over it, drawing out each moment just to look at her. To look at what was finally his. The softness. The sweetness. He kissed her, soothing and arousing her, as he undressed himself. His hands were gentle, because he knew it was what she needed. His mouth was patient, allowing her to set the pace. And the pace was slow and dreamy.

He lowered her to the bed she'd made so neatly that morning, gave himself the quiet delight of brushing her hair with his fingers until it was all tangled golden curls over the plain white quilt. Her eyes were closed, and already her cheeks carried the faint flush of stirred passions.

Last night there had been only the light from a practical and unscented emergency candle, a narrow bunk and a room that smelled of old coffee.

Today there was sunlight, birdsong, and the perfume of the flowers by her window. And today, he thought, she knew there would be pleasure.

He gave her pleasure. Rivers of it. She floated on it, glided on it, immersed herself in it without reserve. All hesitancy, all shyness, vanished under a warm haze of gently lapping sensations.

The texture of his callused fingers, the friction of them as they moved over her skin caused little sparking shocks that speeded her pulse. The taste of his mouth as it moved to her flesh, then back to her lips, was drugging. She could hear his breathing quicken, or those little hums of pleasure in his throat, whenever he touched some new part of her. He was so beautiful to her—not just his incredibly stunning outward good looks. More, it was the beauty inside that drew and seduced her—the kindness, the strength, the patience.

It delighted her to be able to squeeze her hands over his biceps, feel the coil of strength in them, in the muscles of his back. She adored the shape and weight of his body, the way it pressed hers deep into the mattress. The light scrape of his teeth on her shoulder gave her a quick, jittery thrill. To answer it, she nipped at his while her hands grew bold enough to journey down.

He hissed out a breath, jolted. Her eyes flashed open when his head reared up. For an instant, for an eternity, she saw something dark and edgy and dangerous in those moss-green eyes. Something that had her blood leaping high and her pulse scrambling.

He yanked himself back into control, the way he would have yanked a wild dog on a thick leash. His muscles knotted. He could have sworn he felt the sweat burst out of his pores.

"Don't worry." His voice was raw, but he lowered his mouth gently to hers again. "Don't be afraid."

She wanted to tell him she wasn't, couldn't be afraid of him. That she would be afraid of nothing that happened between them. That she wanted to know what had come into his eyes. But he was kissing her into oblivion again, into that misty place where there was nothing but warm, quiet pleasures.

Her moan was long and deep when he eased her to a peak. Long and deep when he gave her more. She let the current take her, opening for him, letting him fill her. Nothing was more stunning than moving with him, feeling his body mesh and mate with hers.

Then his mouth was at her ear, and through her own gasping passion she heard him say her name. Just her name, before he pulled her with him.

"I love you." He still ached for her, even as he shifted his weight and drew her against his side. "I want you to get used to hearing that."

"Devin—"

"No, I don't expect it yet. I will, but I don't expect it yet." He turned his face into her hair and breathed in the scent of it and her, a scent that always reminded him of sunlight on a meadow. "You just get used to hearing it. You tell me when you're used to it, because then I'm going to ask you to marry me."

She went rigid. "I can't. How can I think about that? This is happening too fast."

"Not for me." He wouldn't be angry, he wouldn't even allow himself to be discouraged by the shock in her voice. Instead, he stroked a hand down her arm and spoke with quiet confidence. "I've gotten good at waiting, so I can wait a while longer. But I figured you should know where I'm heading here. I want you, I want the kids, I want a life, but I can wait until you're ready."

"I might never be ready. Devin, you have to understand, I don't know if I can ever make those promises again."

"You've never made them to me. That's all that counts." He rose up on his elbow so that he could study her face. He'd frightened her, he noted. But it couldn't be helped. "I love you. You let that settle in, and we'll see what happens next."

"Don't you see that—"

"I only see you, Cassie." Persuasively, he kissed her, until the hand she'd lifted to' push against his shoulder went lax. "Only you."

A few miles away, Joe Dolin was policing a picnic area on the battlefield for litter. As he worked, his eyes scanned the fields, the hills, the road below. There were large, shady trees, stone walls. He was going to pick his time, and his spot. This wasn't it.

Eventually the crew would work their way down toward the bridge where General Burnside had screwed up during the Battle of Antietam. There the ground was uneven, rocky and thick with brush. There was a creek to hide his scent, trees to cover him.

He'd often poached in those woods, jacklighting deer illegally with some of his drinking buddies. He had plenty of time now to calculate how long it would take him to travel through them, where he could hide, who he could go to for a little help.

In the meantime, he was making himself a busy little bee, picking up the soft drink cans and wrappers tossed aside by lousy tourists or kids hooking school. His supervisor wasn't a fool, but Joe never gave him any lip, any trouble, and made sure he was first in line to volunteer for any of the harder or messier jobs.

He was building himself a damn good rep in prison, something he'd never had on the outside. Something, he thought as he wiped sweat from his brow, that was going to help him get out of the cage.

And get back to Cassie. Get to Cassie.

The little bitch was going to pay for every day he'd spent behind bars. Every hour he'd had to go without a drink or a woman.

When he was finished with her, he was going after MacKade. Maybe all four of the stinking MacKades. He'd had plenty of time to plan it out, to work out the mistakes, to dream about it.

He hoped he had to kill one of them. He hoped it would be Devin. And when he was finished, he was going to Mexico, taking whatever was left of his wife with him.

All he needed was money, a car and a gun. He knew exactly where he was going to get all three.

Chapter 9

Connor tried to take in everything at once. He knew Bryan was getting restless, wandering around the sheriff's office, trying to get a look at the cells in the back. But for himself, he thought nothing was more fascinating than watching the sheriff handle calls and type up reports.

He was going to write a story about it, and he had to get everything just right. The way the office looked, with the dust dancing in the sunlight through the windows, the scars on the desk from feet or cigarettes, the way the ceiling fan squeaked overhead.

He took a deep sniff and filed away in his mind the scent of coffee—really strong, and a little harsh—and the smell of the dust that sort of tickled the nose.

He tried to remember just how the phone sounded when it shrilled on the sheriff's desk, how the sheriff's chair scraped against the floor, how the deputy scratched his head, then his cheek, as he put papers away in the file cabinet.

He already had the sound of the sheriff's voice. It was deep and slow, and there was a hint of something in it. Humor, Connor thought, when he answered some of the calls. Other times it was brisk, kind of official. Once or twice he'd seen lines form between the sheriff's brows.

He sure did drink a lot of coffee, Connor thought, and he wrote a lot of things down. Connor had a million questions, but he held them in because he knew the sheriff was working.

Devin glanced up and saw the boy watching him. Like an owl, he thought. Wise and patient. A look at his watch told him he'd kept the kids hemmed in for most of their Saturday morning. He imagined Connor could sit there, quiet as a mouse, for hours yet. But he recognized the signs of trouble brewing in Bryan.

It was time to give them all a break.

"Donnie, you take over here. We're going to get some lunch at Ed's."

"Yo."

"The state boys call about the Messner case, you tell them I'll have the report to them by Monday."

"Yo," Donnie said again, and crushed his brows together over the filing.

"I'll pick up lunch for Curtis. Tell him, if he starts to make noises back there."

"You got a prisoner?" Suddenly all of Bryan's boredom was washed away in the thrill of it. "You didn't tell us."

"Just somebody sleeping off a night on the town." He was almost sorry he couldn't tell them it was a mad psychopath. "I could use a burger."

"All right!" Bryan darted out of the door. "I'm starving. Extra fries, right, Con?"

"I guess." Connor could hardly think about food with all the questions in his head. "Ah, Sheriff, how come you have that police radio on all the time? I mean, it has fire department stuff, and things from out of your jurisdiction."

"Because you can never be sure what might come over that you'd have to pay attention to."

"When you know somebody, does it feel funny to have to lock them up?"

"Sometimes if you know them it makes it easier to settle things before they get out of hand."

"Have you ever had anybody break out?" Bryan wanted to know as he danced backward on the sidewalk. "Like, conk you over the head and run for it?"

Devin ran his tongue around his teeth. He had a wonderful image of poor old Curtis going over the wall. "Nope, can't say as I have."

"If they did, you'd have to shoot them, right?" The excitement of it leaped in Bryan's eyes. "Like in the leg."

"If they did, it's likely I'd know who they were, so I'd just go to their house and bring them back."

"What if they resisted arrest?"

Devin knew what was expected of him. "I'd have to rough 'em up."

"Slap the cuffs on him," Bryan said with a hoot. "And back into the cage. Wham!"

"The town's quiet," Connor said, "because the sheriff keeps it quiet."

Touched, Devin flipped a finger over the bill of Connor's ball cap. "Thanks. We aim to serve."

"Sheriff."

Devin turned and watched with an inner sigh as the ancient and wiry owner of the general store and sub shop approached. The man could talk the bark off a tree.

"Afternoon, Mr. Grant. How's business?"

"Oh, up and down, Sheriff, up and down." Mr. Grant paused, flicked a bit of lint from the front of his wrinkled brown shirt. "I thought I should let you know, Sheriff...not that I poke my nose into what's not my business... With me, it's live and let live..."

That ended the statement, which Devin knew was habitual. Mr. Grant's mind wandered freely from pillar to post. "Let me know what, Mr. Grant?"

"Oh, well, I was just taking a little air and happened to walk by the bank. Just past closing time, you know."

"Yes, I know."

"Seemed to me somebody was holding up the bank."

"Excuse me?"

"Seemed to me," Mr. Grant repeated, in his ponderous way, "somebody was holding up the bank.

Had a gun, sure enough. Looked to me to be a .45. Could be I'm wrong about that. Might be a .38."

Before either boy could comment, Devin slapped a hand on each of their shoulders. "Go on up to Ed's. Stay there."

"But, Devin—"

"Do it, Bryan. Go on now, both of you. Stay there, and don't say anything." He stared hard at Connor. "Don't say anything," he repeated. "We don't want people getting upset and getting in the way."

"What are you going to do?" Connor said in an awed voice.

"I'm going to take care of it. Get up to Ed's. Move. Now."

When they ran off, Devin kept one eye on them, to be sure they obeyed. "Mr. Grant, I wonder if you'd come along with me. Let's just take a look at this."

"Fine by me."

The bank was across the street and another half a block up. An old brick building with elaborate iron-work, it sat catty-corner from Ed's Café. A quick look showed Devin that the boys had indeed gone in. They had their faces pressed up to the window.

Devin scanned the street. It was Saturday, and there was considerable traffic. Enough, in any case, to cause a problem if there was trouble. He didn't intend to have any of his people hurt.

"Did you get a look at the man, Mr. Grant?"

"Some. Young, 'bout your age, I expect. Can't say as I recognized him. Looked a little like the Harris boy, but wasn't."

Devin nodded. He spotted a dirty white compact with Delaware tags at the curb in front of the bank. "Recognize that car there?"

Mr. Grant thought it over. "Can't say as I do. Never seen it around here."

"Stay here a minute." Unsnapping the flap covering his weapon, Devin sidestepped up to the bank. The door was festooned with curvy ironwork. Through it, he could make out one teller behind the wide counter. And the man across from her, nervously waving a gun.

It was a .45, he noted. Grant had been dead-on.

He slipped away from the door. "Mr. Grant, I'd like you to get on down to the office, tell Donnie I need some backup here at the bank. We've got an armed robbery in progress. I want you to tell him that, straight out. And that I don't want him coming up here blaring sirens or coming into the bank. I don't want him coming into the bank. Have you got that?"

"Why, sure I do, Sheriff. Be happy to oblige."

"And stay down there yourself, Mr. Grant. Don't come back up here."

He'd just started to move again when he saw Rafe approaching. Before his brother could lift a hand in greeting, Devin snagged him. "You're deputized."

"Hell, Devin, Regan just send me out for more diapers. I haven't time to play deputy."

"See that car? White compact, Delaware plates?"

"Sure. I got eyes."

"Put it out of commission."

Now Rafe's brows lifted, and his grin flashed. "Gee, Devin, I don't know as I remember how."

"Do it," Devin said, and the sharp impatience got through.

"What's going on?"

"Somebody's robbing the bank. Put the car out of commission in case he gets past me. And do what you can to keep people out of the way without getting them stirred up."

"You're not going in there alone."

"I've got the gun, you don't," Devin pointed out. "And I've got the badge. Be a pal, Rafe, and deal with the car. As far as I can tell, there's only one perp. I'm going in. If he comes out waving that damn gun, don't be a jerk. Get out of the way."

The hell he would, Rafe thought, but he crouched down to move around to the driver's side of the car while Devin took out his weapon.

Devin wanted to keep it simple, and safe. He tucked his gun into the back of his belt, slipped his badge off and into his pocket. He strolled into the bank, smiled at the teller.

"Hey there, Nancy. Thought I'd be too late to make my deposit. Lucky for me you're still open."

Though her face was frozen in fear, she managed to gape at him. "But— But—"

"The wife'll have my hide if I forget to put the money in. We got that automatic withdrawal on our insurance, you know." He strolled up to the counter, one hand reaching down.

"Are you crazy?" the man with the gun shrieked out, nerves in every syllable. "Are you out of your mind? Get down on the floor! Down! Now!"

"Hey, I'm not butting in line," Devin said reasonably. "Just trying to do some business." He kept his eyes on the man's face, his hand still going down and back, where a man kept his wallet.

"I'll show you some business!"

To Devin's relief, the man shifted the gun from Nancy and toward him. "Put your damn money on the counter. I'll take that, too."

As if he'd just noticed the weapon, Devin held up a hand in peace. "Holy hell, you robbing the bank?"

"What does it look like I'm doing, Einstein? Let's have the money."

"Okay, okay. I don't want any trouble here. You can have it." But instead of his wallet, Devin came out with his gun. "Now, are we going to stand here and shoot each other, or what?"

The man's eyes went wild. "I'll kill you! I swear I'll kill you!"

"That's a possibility." A remote one, since the idiot was waving the gun like a flag on the Fourth of July. "It's just as likely I'll kill you. You drop that gun on the floor and step back from it. You've already got armed robbery, you don't want to add shooting a police officer."

"A cop, a damn cop! Then I'll just shoot her!" Furious, he swung the gun back toward the teller.

Devin didn't hesitate, he didn't even bother to curse. Nancy was just where she should be. On the floor, out of the line of fire. And since he was close enough, Devin used his fist instead of his gun.

"Damn idiot."

The man managed to get off one shot at the ceiling before the gun flew out of his hand. Ignoring it, Devin put his own between the man's eyes.

"What you want to do now," he said calmly, "is roll yourself over and put your hands behind your head. If you don't, I'm going to have to blow your head right off, and this carpet's only a year old."

"Damn cop. Damn lousy one-horse town."

"You got that right." With a bit more force than was strictly necessary, Devin jerked the man's hands down, cuffed them. "You shouldn't mess with small towns. We're real careful about them. Anybody hurt back there? You all right, Nancy?"

As a chorus of breathless, excited voices exploded from behind the counter, he glanced back, knowing Rafe was behind him. And grinned at the crowbar his brother was slapping against his palm.

"I told you I'd handle it."

"This was just in case. What did you do, Dev, scalp him?"

Idly Devin picked up the wig that had been dislodged during the scuffle. "Looks that way. Might as well give him a shave while I'm at it." None too gently, he pulled the man's head back and ripped off the fake moustache. "In case you haven't figured it out, you're under arrest. You have the right to remain silent . . ." he began as he hauled the man to his feet.

He finished Mirandizing him on the way to the door. "Y'all get up from behind there now. I'm going to send Donnie in to get your statements."

From their station at the diner window, both boys watched Devin come out, dragging a balding man with a bloody lip.

"He got him," Bryan said, awed. "Devin got an honest-to-God bank robber."

"Of course he did." Connor beamed. "He's the sheriff."

There was talk of little else but the attempted bank robbery. In the way of small towns, unofficial reports leaped over the wires far ahead of official ones. In many of the phone and backyard-fence conversations, it was said that Devin had burst into the bank, gun drawn, eyes blazing. In others, he had taken out the robber, who'd been armed to the teeth with automatic weapons, bare-handed.

By the end of the day, Devin found himself the recipient of enough homemade baked goods that he could have opened his own restaurant. They made up for the endless official reports he had to type and file. They nearly made up for the phone calls he was forced to field, from concerned citizens, the mayor, the bank manager, and a number of women who thought he might need a bit of comfort after his ordeal.

He was deflecting one of the offers when his brothers walked in.

"No, Annie, I wasn't wounded." He rolled his eyes as all three of his visitors grinned at him. "No, he didn't shoot me. Sharilyn's exaggerating. Ah..." A little baffled by the offer presented to him, he cleared his throat. "That's nice of you, Annie, and I appreciate the thought, but— No, I don't think I'm going to suffer from delayed stress syndrome. Yeah, I've heard of it, but— No, no, really, I'm just fine. And I'm a little tied up right now. Yeah, official business. That's right. You take care now. Uh-huh. You bet. Bye.''

He let out a long breath, shaking his head briskly as he replaced the receiver. "Holy hell."

"Was that Annie 'The Body' Linstrom?" Shane wanted to know.

"She was hitting on me," Devin said with a snort of laughter. "Women are a puzzle. There's no way around it."

Jared sat on the corner of Devin's desk. "The way I heard it, bullets bounce off your chest."

"Nah." Shane sniffed at one of the pies sitting on a crowded shelf. "I heard he eats bullets. Betty Malloy bake this lemon meringue?"

"Yeah." Devin winced when the phone rang again. "Where the hell is Donnie?"

"Last I saw, he was strutting down Main Street trying to look like Supercop." Rafe cocked his head. "Aren't you going to answer it—Sheriff?"

Devin swore and picked up the phone. "Sheriff's office. MacKade."

He leaned back, closed his eyes. It was the press again. Every small paper and news bureau within fifty miles had picked up on the botched robbery. By rote, he gave the official line, danced around the demand for a more in-depth interview, and hung up.

"You're good at that," Jared decided. "Real stern and authoritative."

"I'm beginning to wish I'd kicked that jerk in the head," Devin muttered. "He's caused me a lot of trouble. Now I'm stuck here, answering the damn phone, typing reports, with some out-of-town idiot who couldn't hold up a lemonade stand in the back. He whines all the time."

"At least you won't starve," Shane said, and helped himself to one of the cookies on a plate by the pie. "We thought we'd take you down to Duff's, buy you a drink."

"Can't leave the prisoner unattended."

"Rough," Jared said, without sympathy. "You know, Bryan was about to jump out of his socks when he got home. You're better than Rambo."

Amused, Devin scratched his cheek: "Don't tell him the last robbery I had to deal with was when a couple of kids stole underwear off Mrs. Metz's clothesline." He shuffled papers on his desk. "Have you been by the inn, Rafe? Everything okay there?"

"Everything's fine. Cassie was a little upset. Word travels," he added unnecessarily. "But I told her it was all blown out of proportion, and you didn't do anything much."

"Thanks a lot."

"No problem. Connor was already writing a story about you."

"No kidding?" The grin all but split his face.

"'A Day in the Life of Sheriff MacKade.'" Rafe helped himself to coffee. "The boy's nuts about you."

"Good thing." Shane took another cookie. "Since Devin's going to marry his mama."

Rafe bobbled the coffee, spilled it on his hand and swore. "Cassie? Little Cassie?"

"Shane's getting ahead of himself," Devin said, in a mild tone that belied the gleam in his eye. "As usual."

"Hey, you're the one who said it. Me, I figure you've just lost your mind. Like these two."

"Shut up, Shane." Jared kept his eyes on Devin's face. "You and Cassie?"

"So what?"

"So... that's interesting."

"Are you speaking as her attorney?" Devin pushed back from the desk. If the phone rang again, he thought he might just rip it out of the wall. To get himself back under control, he went to the coffee.

"He's got it bad," Rafe observed. "Didn't you have a thing for her about ten, twelve years ago?" When Devin didn't answer, merely poured the coffee, sipped it steely-eyed, Rafe grinned. "Never got over it, did you? Son of a gun. Why, that's practically poetic, bro. It gets me, right here." He thumped a hand on his chest.

"Keep ragging me, it'll get you somewhere else."

"It's getting so every day's Valentine's Day in Antietam." In disgust, Shane shoved another cookie in his mouth. "A man's not safe."

"Cassie's a sweetheart," Rafe said pointedly.

"Sure she is." Gamely, Shane swallowed, so that he could make his point. "She's as good as they come, and pretty with it. But why does that mean he has to marry her? You see all this stuff?" With a sweep of his hand, he indicated all the pies, cakes, tarts, cookies.

178 The Heart of Devin MacKade

"Women are going to fall all over him, and he's toss-ing them off because he's gone cross-eyed over *one* woman. It's not only stupid, it's . . . well, it's selfish."

Rafe gave Shane a thump on the back of the head that would have felled a grizzly. "Man, I love this guy. He's going to carry the MacKade legend into the next millennium."

"Damn right," Shane agreed. "No woman's going to tie me down. I mean, with all the flowers out there, why pick one when you can have a bouquet?"

"Now that's poetry." Rafe thumped him again. "Let's go get that beer."

"You two go on." Jared stayed where he was. "I need to talk to Devin a minute."

They left, arguing about who was buying. When the room was quiet again, Devin took his coffee back to his desk. "You got a problem?"

"No." Jared shifted so that they were face-to-face. "But you might. Have you talked to Cassie about marriage?"

"A little. Why?"

"Joe Dolin."

"They're divorced. It's done."

"They're divorced." Eyes steady, Jared rested a hand on his knee. "But done's another thing. He'll get out eventually, Devin. He'll come back."

"I'll handle it."

"Yeah, I figure you can handle Joe, one-on-one. But there's the law."

Unconsciously Devin brushed a finger over his badge. "He tries to touch Cassie again, just tries, and I'll have him back behind bars before he can blink."

"And that's part of the problem. You're the sheriff, but you won't be objective. You can't be."

Devin set his coffee aside, leaned forward. "I've been in love with her most of my life. At least it seems that way. And I had to stand back and do little more than nothing while he hurt her. While I knew what he was doing to her inside that house. She wouldn't let me help, so the law tied my hands. Things are different now, and nothing's going to stop me from taking care of her. He lifts his hand to her again, and he's dead. Problem solved."

Jared nodded. He didn't take the statement lightly. He knew what it was to need to protect the woman you loved from any sort of harm. And he knew Devin was a man who said exactly what he meant.

"I'm talking about a situation that could develop if he's smart enough not to lift his hand to her. What if, after he serves his time, he moves back here, stays clean. How are you going to handle that?"

"One step at a time, Jared, like always. Of course, the first thing I'd have to do is keep Rafe from going after him because of what he tried to do to Regan."

That was true enough, Jared thought. And Rafe wouldn't be the only one who wouldn't welcome Joe Dolin back into the community. "Dev, I know what Cassie's been through. Exactly. I know because I'm her lawyer, I handled the divorce. We're talking about a textbook case of spousal abuse. A pitiful phrase, *textbook case,* for that kind of horror. Therapy's helped her, the town's helped her, and her own backbone's helped her. But she's got scars she's never going to get rid of."

"I'm being careful," Devin said slowly. "For God's sake, Jared, I've given her time—even after the divorce, I waited and gave her time. I'm trying to give her more."

"Devin, I'm just trying to show you the whole package. Believe me, I can't think of anyone I'd rather see you with than Cassie. Anyone I'd rather see her with than you. God knows she deserves somebody decent. But it's not just the two of you. There are two kids here. Joe Dolin's kids."

Devin's eyes darkened, narrowed. "You can say that to me, when you've got Bryan? Are you going to tell me it matters they're another man's blood, when I know damn well Bryan's as much yours as Layla?"

"That's not what I'm saying." Jared's voice was low and calm. "I've seen you with them. I didn't have a clue how you felt about Cassie. You kept that covered well. But anybody with eyes can see you're crazy about those kids, that you've been good for both of them. They deserve you," he added, and nipped Devin's temper before it could bloom. "They deserve a father who loves them, and a home where they can just be kids."

"Fine. That's what I'm going to see they have."

"But it's not like Bryan, Dev. His biological father isn't around, isn't an issue. Dolin is."

"He doesn't give a damn about those kids, never has."

"No, but he'll have a right to them." Knowing that the frustration he felt didn't help, Jared spread his hands and took a deep breath. "The law says he does. And if he can't get to Cassie, he may just come up with the notion to get to her through them. Once he's out, he'll have a legal right to see them, to have visitation, to be part of their lives. You won't be able to block that."

Devin hadn't thought of it. Maybe he hadn't let himself. Now that it was there, right in the front of his mind, his blood went cold. "You're the lawyer. You block it."

"Parental rights are a sticky business, Dev. You know that. Until and unless he does something to put them in jeopardy, until and unless we can prove he's not just unfit, but dangerous to them, he'll have the law on his side."

Already Devin was thinking it through, working it out. "We may be able to put the pressure on for supervised visitations only, but blood still counts heavy in court."

"He beat Connor."

Jared's brows drew together. "I didn't know anything about that."

"Connor didn't tell Cassie, didn't want to make it worse on her."

"I might be able to use that, if the time comes. But once he's considered rehabilitated, a lot of the slate gets erased. He's going to be in for a long time yet, but I want you to know what you're up against here."

"I've got a clear picture of what I'm up against. Nothing's going to stop me from making Cassie and the kids mine. Not Joe Dolin, not the law, not anything."

"Well, then." Jared rose. "I'll state the obvious. I'm behind you. Rafe and Shane are behind you."

"I appreciate it."

"If you get yourself out from behind that desk for an hour, come down to Duff's. I'll buy you a beer." Satisfied, Jared headed for the door, then paused. "She's a terrific woman, Dev. Sweet, like Shane says, but tougher than you might think. Tougher than she thinks. If you convince her she wants you as much as you want her, you'll handle whatever comes down. I've got one piece of advice."

"You always do," Devin said dryly.

"For Cassie, it's not enough to let her know you love her, you want her. You let her know you need her. That's a woman who'd go to the wall for a man who needed her."

He did need her, Devin thought when Jared had shut the door behind him. But he didn't know how to show her, and wasn't entirely sure he should. Wasn't that just the kind of pressure he was struggling not to put on her?

He didn't want Cassie to go to the wall for him. He only wanted her to feel safe and happy. No, it was up to him to see that she was never hurt again, to protect her, to shield her and the children.

His need could wait.

Chapter 10

Cassie told herself it was foolish to worry. Devin was fine. Rafe had told her the story himself, and she knew that his version of the attempted bank robbery was much more accurate than those she'd heard over the phone. Even Connor's report, given in fits and starts of desperate excitement, had been less dramatic than the gossip spewing out of the town.

So there was no need to worry.

She was so worried, she jumped each time the phone rang. If she'd been able to leave the inn and the children for an hour, she'd have dashed into town to check every inch of Devin herself.

One thought, one fact, kept running in a loop in her brain. He'd faced down a man with a gun.

She shuddered again, and gave up trying to block the picture from her mind. He'd walked into an armed robbery, risked his life to protect others. His badge had never taken on such huge proportions for her before. He'd risked his life. In the day-to-day business of a town like Antietam, a sheriff's work was more diplomacy—or so she'd imagined—than risk.

Of course, now, she began to see that had been foolish of her. There were fights, drunks, break-ins, hot tempers between neighbors and families. She had personal knowledge of the dangers of domestic disputes—that tidy term for the violence that could happen behind closed doors.

He was in charge. And while Connor might see him as a hero, she began to see just how vulnerable the badge made him.

Because she did, she also realized that the worry that ate at her all through the long afternoon and evening wasn't just for a friend, a lover, not just for a man she admired and cared for. It was for the man she loved.

It had taken something unexpected, shocking, to open her eyes. Now that they were open, she could look back. Almost as far back as she could remember, Devin had been there. She had depended on him, admired him and in some ways, she supposed, taken his place in her life for granted.

It had been humiliating to go to him and admit what Joe had done to her, to show him the marks, to describe how she had come by them. Not just because he'd been the sheriff, she thought now. Because he had been Devin.

She'd always been more shy around him than around his brothers. Because, she thought again, he'd been Devin. Part of her heart had always been set aside for him. So she had never been able to look at him as just one of the MacKades, or just her friend, or just the sheriff.

She'd always felt something more. Now she was free, and she could let those feelings out. She could admit that it wasn't just part of her heart that belonged to him, but all of it.

All of her.

Through the worry came the wonder, and with it the joy. She loved.

When the phone rang, she raced to it like a madwoman, then struggled to keep her voice calm when Savannah greeted her.

"Hi, I guess you've heard the big news by now."

"No one's talking about anything else." To calm herself, Cassie reached over to the refrigerator and took out a pitcher of juice. "Have you seen Devin since it happened?"

"Not personally. Jared has. He says our big, bad sheriff is annoyed with all the glory. A television crew came down from Hagerstown, and the paper's been here." Because she understood Cassie's silence perfectly, she softened her voice. "He's fine, Cassandra. Not a scratch. Just grumbling because this whole business is going to keep him tied up for a while. Are you all right?"

"Me?" Cassie stared at the juice she'd poured. "I'm fine. I'm just concerned."

"I know. I have to admit that by the time Bryan finished giving me the play-by-play, I was pretty concerned myself. But the one thing we can all be sure of is that Devin MacKade can handle himself."

"Yes." Cassie picked up the glass, set it down again. "He can. I guess there's no one who needs anyone worrying about him less than Devin." But why hadn't he called?

"Listen, I really called to ask you a favor."

"Sure. What can I do?"

"You can give my temper a break and send Connor over for the night. Bryan's been nagging me since he got home from the great bank robbery."

"Oh." Cassie peeked out the window into the yard, where Connor and Emma were playing with the cat. "He'd love it, if you're sure."

There was a crash, and Cassie could hear Savannah yell, "Bryan MacKade, if you break a window with that baseball, you're not only out of the game, you're suspended for the season!

"Yes, I'm sure," she said to Cassie, with feeling, when she returned to talk in the receiver. "But there's more. Can we have Emma, too?"

"Emma? You want Emma to spend the night?"

"Jared has this idea that we'd better start practicing with girls. We sure know boys, and he started thinking that once Layla starts growing up, we'll be lost." She laughed, and Cassie heard the baby coo. "So, how about giving us Emma for the experiment? We swear we'll turn her back over in one piece."

"She'd be thrilled. But, Savannah, you'd have four to deal with."

"Yeah. We've decided that's our magic number. If you know what I mean."

"Four?" It was Cassie's turn to chuckle. "Well, you're going to need plenty of practice, then."

"Let's just see how we survive one night. Pack them up, will you, Cassie? Jared will walk over through the woods and get them."

"On one condition. You'll call, anytime, if you want to bail out."

"You've got my word on that one." There was another crash, and something shattered. "All right, Bryan, now you have to die. Hurry, Cassie—I have to believe there's safety in numbers."

Though it tugged at her heart a little, Cassie supervised the overnight packing, while her children bristled with excitement. They were so eager to go, and she tried not to fret that it was Emma's first sleepover.

She made certain they had clean clothes, toothbrushes, instructions on how to behave. They even took the cat. When they trooped off toward the woods with Jared, she was completely, utterly alone.

With too much time, she realized, to think, to brood, to worry.

She went down to the inn, found the handful of guests well occupied and content. Still, she set up cake and coffee in the parlor, offered complimentary wine to those playing cards in the sunroom.

Seeing that she wasn't needed, she set the table for breakfast, and checked her pantry and refrigerator, though she knew she was well supplied for the large Sunday breakfast the inn was becoming renowned for.

At loose ends, she wandered outside. She wasn't used to having nothing to do, no one to look after. Certainly, she had often fantasized about how she would spend an evening alone. A bubble bath, a book, a late movie on television.

That was what she would do, she told herself. As soon as she ran into town and made sure Devin was really fine.

She dashed up the stairs, then let out a yelp when she saw the shadowy figure on the porch swing.

"I saw you were busy," Devin said. "Thought I'd wait."

She still had a hand against her speeding heart. "I thought you had to stay in town."

"I dragooned Donnie into staying at the office. It's the least he can do, after he left me with the phones all damn afternoon." He held out a bouquet of yellow tea roses. "I brought you flowers. I was going by the florist and remembered I'd never brought you flowers. I know you like them."

"They're beautiful."

"Are you going to sit down with me?"

"All right." She sat and held the roses in her arms as she would have a child. "They're beautiful," she said again. "I should put them in water."

"They'll keep a minute." Curious, he tucked a hand under her chin and turned her face to his. "What is it?"

"It's nothing. I was so worried," she blurted out. "I couldn't leave, and kept waiting for you to call. Devin, why didn't you call? I'm sorry," she said immediately. "I shouldn't nag you."

One of the scars, he mused, and kept his fingers firm when she would have looked away. "Don't be sorry. I did call, several times. Your phone was busy."

"Everyone's been calling. I've heard a dozen different stories."

"The truth's probably less exciting."

"He had a gun, didn't he? You knew he had a gun when you went into the bank."

"I had to do my job, Cass. He wasn't going to get anywhere, and even if he did, there was a canister inside the moneybag that would have spewed red paint all over him and the bills." His grin spread. "Actually, I'm kind of sorry we couldn't play that part out. It would have been some show. But he might have hurt someone."

"He might have hurt you."

"Well, then, you didn't hear about how bullets bounce off me."

Instead of laughing, she pressed her face into his shoulder. "I'm so glad you're all right. I'm so glad you're not hurt. I'm so glad you're here."

"I'm happy to be all of those things." Slipping an arm around her, he set the swing in motion. "I'd have come sooner, if I could."

"I know. You were on the news."

"Yeah. So I hear."

"You didn't see." She turned her head. "They'll show it again at eleven."

"I know what I look like."

Studying his face, she found something endearing. "You're embarrassed."

"No, I'm not." He shifted. "Maybe. Some."

Not just endearing, she realized. Adorable. "I'm awfully proud of you," she murmured, and brushed her lips over his. "Actually, we taped the broadcast. Connor was so excited. We can watch it, if you want."

"I'll pass. I don't—"

She interrupted him with her lips again, and experienced an odd, sweet power when she felt his heart jump. "I've watched it three times. I thought you looked like a movie star."

"You don't get out enough." His palms were damp, so he eased off the swing. A little distance, MacKade, he warned himself, before you explode. "I've been thinking about that, too. I haven't ever taken you out. To dinner, or anywhere."

"You took us down to the zoo in the spring, and to the fair last summer."

Why was she looking at him like that? he wondered. She'd never looked at him like that before. With... Was that amusement, or lust, or— God.

"I meant you and me. I love having the kids, but—"

"I don't have to go out on dates, Devin. I'm happy with the way things are."

"Still and all." He couldn't seem to think very clearly, not when she was just sitting here, smiling at him, a bouquet of flowers in her arms. "I, ah, brought all this food. Pies and cookies and cakes. People have been bringing them by the office all afternoon."

"They're grateful." With her heart tripping lightly, she rose. "They want to show it."

"Yeah, well, I'd never be able to eat it all. I gave some to Donnie, but I figured the kids might..." He backed up when she stepped forward. "They might want some. I didn't see them when I came up. It's a little early for them to be in bed on a Saturday night, isn't it?"

"They're not here." She blessed Savannah and Jared, and fate. "They're spending the night at the cabin."

"They're not here."

"No. We're alone."

He'd been prepared to leave, to spend a little time with her, then go. He wouldn't have asked to stay with her through the night, with the children in the next room. None of them were ready for that.

Now they were alone, and the night had just begun. A slap of desire whipped through him, painfully. He braced against it, and managed an easy smile.

"Then I'll take you out."

"I don't want you to take me out," she murmured. "I want you to take me to bed."

It closed his throat. "Cassie." His hand was very gentle on her cheek. "I don't expect that every time I come here. That's not the only reason I want to be with you."

"I know." She turned her lips into his palm. "It's what I'd like tonight. I'm going to put these in water."

She left him, churning and speechless, on the dark porch. More than a little dazed, he followed her inside.

"I bought this at Regan's shop." Briskly Cassie filled a green depression-glass pitcher with water. "I'm still getting used to having a little extra money to buy pretty things. I don't even feel guilty about it anymore."

"You shouldn't feel guilty about anything."

"Oh, a few things." With hands as gentle as they were efficient, she arranged the roses in the pitcher. "But not this. And not you." Her eyes lifted. "Do you know what I feel about you, Devin? About us?"

He thought it was best not to try to speak just then, not with the way the blood was draining out of his head.

"Dazzled," she murmured. "You dazzle me. You make me feel things, and want things I never knew I could have. I'm almost twenty-nine, and you're the only man who's really touched me. I want you to touch me."

He would, as soon as he could be sure he had his hands, and his needs, under control. If it had been anyone but Cassie, he would have thought she was seducing him.

Because he said nothing, made no move toward her, she was afraid she was doing it all wrong. It wasn't nerves now that plagued her, so much as doubt. And doubt had her shifting her gaze back to the flowers.

"If you'd rather not right now... if you don't want me—"

"God." It exploded out of him, made her head whip up in alarm, made him bite back whatever might have come out next. "Let's go for a drive," he said quickly. "It's a pretty night, the moon's coming up. I'd like to go for a drive with you."

She was sure she'd made some foolish mistake, but couldn't put her finger on it. All she was sure of was that her system was in overdrive, and his wasn't. As a seductress, she thought, she was a miserable amateur.

"All right, if you like."

He recognized that tone, the bright and false cheer-fulness. He would have slit his throat before he did anything to cause that. "Cassie, it's not that I don't want to make love with you. I do. It's just that... Maybe I'm a little more revved from this morning than I thought. I need to smooth out some of the edges before I... I can't touch you now," he ended, his tone too sharp, too quick.

"Why?"

"Because I'm a little too needy right now, and it doesn't help for you to keep looking at me that way. I wouldn't be able to— I'd hurt you."

"You're angry with me?"

"No." He swore, ripely, showing her some portion of his frustration in the way he whirled around and paced. "When I'm angry with you, you'll know it. You're driving me crazy. Look at the way you're standing there, with your hands folded and those big, gorgeous eyes watching every move I make. I can't breathe when you look at me like that. I used to be able to." He shot the words out like an accusation. "But that was before, and I just can't handle it as well now that we've been together. We've got to get out of here before I eat you alive."

"We're not going anywhere." It surprised them both, how firm and settled her voice.

"I'm telling you—"

"Yes, I believe you are trying to tell me. You think I'm too fragile to handle it. To handle you. Well, you're wrong."

"You haven't got a clue what you're dealing with, not with me."

"Maybe I don't. Maybe you haven't let me." Suddenly strong, suddenly sure, she walked to him. "Every time we've made love, it hasn't been for you."

"Don't be ridiculous. Of course it was for me."

"It was for me," she said firmly. Strong, she thought. Strong face, strong eyes, strong hands. Not a picture in a magazine, or a white knight fantasy. A strong man, with strong needs. "You were so careful, so patient. No one's ever been careful with me before."

"I know." Because he did, his hand was gentle when he lifted it to brush the golden curls of her hair. "You don't have to worry anymore."

"Don't treat me like a child, Devin." Boldly she took his face in her hands, that familiar and compelling face. "You were holding back. Every time, you were holding back. I've been too dazzled to realize it."

"Cassie, you need tenderness."

"Don't tell me what I need." Her voice had a snap to it, there was a spark in her eyes. "I've had enough of that in my life. Yes, I need tenderness, but I also need trust and respect, and to be treated like a woman. A normal woman."

As carefully as he could, he wrapped his fingers around her wrists. "Don't push me here, Cassie." He pressed his lips to her brow, and infuriated her.

"Kiss me like you mean it," she demanded, then crushed her lips to his. She felt his jolt, the burst of heat, then his struggle for control. "Show me what it's like," she said against his mouth. "I want to know what it's like, what you're like when you stop thinking."

With an oath, he devoured her mouth. It was like that first shocking kiss, she realized as her blood burst inside her veins. The first and the last time he had given her a glimpse of real hunger.

There was that surge of power again, that odd, whippy sensation that she could do or be anything. She strained against him when he tried to draw back.

"Damn it, Cassie."

"Again." Surprisingly strong, she dragged his dark head back to hers. "Kiss me like that again." Her eyes, slumberous, aware, stayed on his. "Show me what it's like," she murmured. "I've waited my whole life to know." She ran her hands over his chest, felt the wild beat of his heart, the rigid edge of his control. "Take me. Don't be kind tonight, Devin. Just take me. That's what I want."

His hands, shaking now, were tensed and rough as he wrapped her hair around them and dragged her head back. He plundered her mouth, ravishing it with lips and teeth and tongue. A part of him hung back still, waiting for her to object. He told himself he would stop—could stop—the moment he frightened her.

But as her taste seeped into him, he was afraid it was a lie. Just look at her, he thought, the sunbeam hair, the cloudy eyes, the rose petal skin.

"Cassie—"

"No. Just show me." She was almost delirious with new knowledge, with the force of her desire and her utter lack of fear. "Show me."

He could have sworn he heard himself snap, heard an echo of brittle control breaking. The wildness overcame him, primitive, almost brutal, making all the years of patience nothing.

In his rush to taste her flesh, he ripped her blouse. The sound of the seam tearing would have snapped him back, but she moaned and wrapped herself around him. Instinctively he recognized the quiver of her body as desire, not fear. It clawed at him.

"I can't . . . stand it."

"Then don't," she murmured, thrilling when his arms clamped around her, when he lifted her off her feet so that she was pressed hard against him, heat to heat. "Touch me." She fisted her pale hands in his dark hair, amazed at the hunger that swarmed through her. "I'll go crazy if you don't."

Nearly stumbling, his mouth racing over her face and throat, he headed for the bedroom. But she wrapped her legs tight around his waist and shot new fire into his blood. By the doorway, he pressed her against the wall, using it to brace her. His desperate mouth clamped over her breast, suckling hard through her tattered blouse. Her response was to throw back her head and rock against him.

"More." She couldn't believe what was coming out of her mouth, couldn't believe this vicious need had been in either one of them. With a groan, she reached down and tore her own blouse aside so that his mouth could take her.

She climaxed the instant his teeth closed over her, shocking herself with the power of it. For an instant she was like a moth, pinned, quivering helplessly, and then she was alive, bursting with life.

Mindless as coupling animals, they dragged each other to the floor.

She pulled at his shirt, he yanked at her slacks. Speech was impossible as they rolled over the floor in the narrow hallway, groping for each other. There were only gasps and moans. No sighs now, no murmurs, only hissing breath and thundering pulses.

Craving drove him, a craving long suppressed and denied. He yanked her hips high and ripped her practical cotton panties to shreds. And made her scream with his greedy mouth.

She bucked, then stiffened into a quaking bridge, her arms straining as her body arched up toward him. He drove her ruthlessly, relentlessly, until throaty growls rumbled in her throat.

"More." This time it was he who demanded it, he who groaned, as her nails scraped up his back and dug crescents into his shoulders. When her hand closed around him, his vision grayed, and the drumbeat of his pulse scrambled.

She was moving under him, writhing. Her eyes were nearly black, and blind with pleasure, when he fused his mouth to hers again. It was greed, rather than control, that kept him from ending it, that had him sliding sleekly down her body again, tasting and taking and touching until they were both mad.

He reared up, clamped his hands over hers, then plunged into her. Beyond all reason, he pumped and thrust, angling her rocking hips so that he could immerse himself in her, deep, then deeper. His mind had gone dark, leaving only snarling sensations as he

rammed into that hot, wet pleasure with a feral force
that had them both gasping.

She couldn't hold on. She tried, for him. How could
she have known he needed like this? That she was capable of needing like this? How could she have known
until he finally showed her? But she was being tossed
too high now to fight her way back. Her hands slid off
his damp skin, rapped hard on the wooden floor. She
gave herself willingly to the last savage stab of pleasure, going weak as he continued to hammer himself
into her.

Then that wonderful hard body heaved, went rigid.
She saw him throw his head back as if in pain, saw
with wonder that it was he who was lost. When he
shuddered, shuddered and cried out her name, she
wept with the joy of it.

He felt the tears against his shoulder the moment his
sated body collapsed on hers. He would have levered
himself away instantly, but her arms came around
him.

"Don't. Please don't move."

"I'm sorry." There was nothing he could say to her
that would be good enough, nothing he could say to
himself that would be bad enough. "I hurt you. I
promised I wouldn't."

"Do you know what you did?" Her lips were
curved, but he couldn't see. All he could see was his
own careless treatment of the most precious thing in
his life. "You forgot."

"Forgot?" Again he tried to shift, again she held
him tight.

"You forgot to be careful, you forgot to worry, you forgot everything. I didn't know I could make you do that. It makes me feel—" a long, satisfied sigh "—powerful."

"Powerful?" His throat was bone-dry. He wanted to lift her up off the floor. God, he'd taken her on the floor. He wanted to tuck her into bed and soothe her. But the word she'd used, and the tone, baffled him.

"Strong, sexy." At last she lifted her arms, stretched them above her head in a long, lazy movement. "Powerful. I've never felt powerful before. I like it. Oh, I really like it." Eyes closed, lips curved, she hummed in her throat.

And that was his first glimpse of her when he lifted his head, the smug smile and erotic glow of a woman who'd just discovered a dangerous and exciting secret. His blood stirred all over again. She looked... triumphant, he realized. Just who, he wondered, had ravaged who?

"You like it," he repeated.

"Mmm... I want to feel this way again. And again and again. I want to feel cherished, too, the way I do when you're gentle. I want to feel everything. I made you forget." She opened her eyes again and laughed when she saw the stunned and sated look in his eyes. "I seduced you. Didn't I?"

"You destroyed me. I tore your clothes."

"I know. It was exciting. Will you do it again?"

"I..." He shook his head, but when it didn't clear he gave up and lost himself in her eyes. "Anytime."

"Can I rip yours?"

Words failed him. He managed a couple of strangled sounds before clearing his throat. "We'd better get off the floor."

"I like it here. I like knowing you wanted me so much you couldn't wait." She lifted a hand to toy with the dark curls that fell, damp, over his forehead. "I like the way you're looking at me right now. It's probably wrong, and I don't care, but I like knowing you wanted me for years. That you watched me, and wanted me. Like this."

"I didn't exactly picture it like this."

Her lips curved again, a sly, knowing smile that made his blood swim. "Didn't you?"

"Well, maybe." His brain was still numb. It was the only part of him that seemed to have shut down. "Once in a while."

She pressed her lips together, ran the tip of her tongue over them. "I can still taste you."

"Oh, God."

A quick and delicious tremor coursed through her as she felt him move inside her. "I'm doing it again."

"Huh?"

"Seducing you."

He couldn't get his breath. "Looks like that."

She felt powerfully a woman, a normal, competent, well-loved woman. "Tell me you love me, Devin. While you're filling me, while you're wanting me, tell me you love me."

He couldn't keep himself from hardening again, from driving deep into her, from groaning as her body rose and fell with him.

"I love you." Helpless, he buried his face in her hair. Somehow she'd taken the reins from him. He could do nothing but ride. "I can't stop."

She absorbed it all, the love, the passion, the power, willingly matching his fast and desperate pace. When she knew he was falling off the edge with her, when they were each defenseless, she turned her lips to his ear.

"I love you, Devin. I love you. I think I always have."

When he could speak again, he gathered her up, cradled her in his lap. "I've wanted to hear that for a long time."

"I meant it. I couldn't have said it unless I did."

"I know." And it left him shaken and without defenses. "You've tossed my master plan into the Dumpster, Cass."

"How?"

"Well, I had it plotted out, you see. By my reckoning, I'd get you to fall in love with me by Christmas. Then I'd keep things at a nice, steady pace, and talk you into marrying me by spring."

"Let's not talk about marriage, Devin. Not yet. Not now."

He tipped her head back. "When?"

"I don't know." There was worry in her eyes again, and in her voice. "Marriage isn't always the right answer."

"It is for people like you and me." He nearly spoke of the children, but stopped himself. It wasn't right to use them to press his case. "I'd make you happy."

"I know you would." She turned her face into the curve of his neck. "Let this be enough for now. It's so much more than I ever thought I'd have. Let it be enough for now."

"For now." He contented himself with the scent of her hair. "Why don't we do this? Get ourselves some wine, some of that pie, have a little picnic?"

"I'd like that." She leaned back, smiled. "I'll get a couple of plates." But when she reached for her slacks, his hand closed over hers.

"You're not going to need those," he said, his eyes dark and wicked.

She laughed. "I'm not going to serve pie buck-naked." Then she blinked, felt a quick skitter of her pulse. "Am I?"

"Why don't we see?"

Chapter 11

School was out, and that made life for two ten-year-old boys close to perfect. The haunted woods that fringed between Bryan's cabin and the inn beckoned. There they could search for ghosts, listen for the pounding of mortar fire, or hunt for more tangible remnants of war in the dirt and brambles. Even after more than a century, old shells could be unearthed.

Connor had a collection Bryan envied, stubby bullets that looked like they were made of clay, an old brass button that had survived the uniform it belonged to and, best of all, the metal triangle of a stirrup Cassie had unearthed in the garden of the inn.

The boys had decided it had belonged to a Union general and his trusty steed.

Connor viewed this stretch of summer in a way he never had before. The last year had been exciting when they moved into the new apartment, but he'd still worried often that it would all end. Now he'd come to believe, now he could anticipate the long, hot days, the companionship of his best friend and a home where no one stumbled in drunk with fists raised.

He watched his mother still. Her eyes no longer looked so tired, and she laughed so much more than she had ever laughed before. He liked the way she put pretty things around the house, the flowers, the pale green glass she'd begun to collect from Regan's shop. But he kept quiet about that, because he knew the guys would rag on him for liking something as lame as flowers or glass bowls.

But not Bryan. Bryan was the best of friends, and didn't even mind if Emma tagged along with them. Bryan liked to listen to Connor's stories. Bryan could keep secrets. Bryan was his brother, his blood brother. They had held a solemn ceremony in the woods, pricking their fingers and mixing their blood together to seal the bond.

They spent some of those early days of freedom from books and classrooms in the tree house Jared had built on the edge of the woods nearest the cabin. Some they spent in the yard of the inn, practicing baseball. They would also cut through the trees and visit Shane at the farm. As Bryan said, Shane was very cool, and he never minded if they wanted to play with the dogs and the puppies or hang out in the hayloft of the big old barn.

But almost every day, it was the woods that pulled at them. And tonight they had finally wangled permission to camp out, just the two of them, deep in the haunted woods.

They had pitched Devin's old tent. It was Devin, Connor knew, who had turned the tide. His mother had worried over the idea of letting the two boys loose for a night, but Devin had talked to her about rites of passage and memories and friendships. He owed the most important night of his life to Sheriff MacKade.

They had built a fire carefully, in a circle of stones on clear ground, as Devin had shown them, and they had hot dogs and marshmallows to roast over it. Cassie had given them a big jug of juice, but Devin had slipped them a six-pack of soda and told them to take the empty cans, along with the other trash, over to the farm in the morning for disposal.

Their sleeping rolls were spread out in the tent, the moon was high and bright overhead, and owls were hooting. The fire crackled, and the scent of scorched meat stung the night air. The sweet, gooey taste of marshmallow was in Connor's mouth. And he was in heaven.

"This is the best," he said.

"It's pretty cool." Bryan watched his hot dog turn black on the end of his stick, just the way he liked it. "We should do it every night."

Connor knew it wouldn't be special if they did it every night, but didn't say so. "It's great here. Sheriff MacKade said that he and his brothers used to camp out in the woods all the time."

"Dad likes to walk in the woods." Bryan loved using that word. *Dad.* He tried to use it often, without making it a big deal. "Mom, too. They sure kiss a lot." He made smacking noises with his lips so Connor would laugh. "Beats me why kissing's supposed to be so damn neat. I think I'd gag if a girl tried to put her mouth on me. Disgusting."

"Revolting. Especially the tongue part."

At that, Bryan executed very realistic vomiting sounds that had both boys rolling with laughter.

"Shane's always kissing girls." Connor rolled his eyes. "I mean, *always.* I heard your dad say he's got an addiction."

Bryan snorted at that. "It's weird. I mean, Shane knows all there is to know about animals and machines and stuff, but he likes having girls hang around. He gets this funny look in his eye, too. Like Devin does with your mom. I figure some girls must zap some guys' brains. Like a laser beam."

"What do you mean?" Connor had gone very still.

"You know, zap!" Bryan demonstrated with a pointed finger and cocked thumb.

"No, about Sheriff MacKade, and my mom."

"Jeez, he's really stuck on her." The hot dog was thoroughly burned. Concentrating, Bryan blew on the end before biting in and filling his mouth with charcoal. "He hangs around her all the time and brings her flowers and junk. That's what my Dad did with Mom. He'd bring her flowers, and she'd go real dopey over them." He shook his head. "Screwy."

"He comes around because he's looking out for us," Connor said, but the sweet taste in his mouth had gone sour. "Because he's the sheriff."

"Sure, he looks out for you." Involved with his hot dog, Bryan didn't see the panic in his pal's eyes.

"Maybe that's how he got stuck on her in the first place, but man, he's gone. I heard my mom and dad talking the other night, and Mom said how she got a kick out of seeing the big, bad sheriff—that's what she calls him—out of seeing him cow-eyed over Cassie. *Cow-eyed.*" Bryan snickered at the term. "Hey, if they get married, we'd be cousins *and* blood brothers. That'd be great."

"She's not getting married." Connor's voice lashed out so fast and furious that Bryan nearly bobbled the rest of his dinner.

"Hey—"

"She's not going to marry anyone, ever again." Connor leaped to his feet, fists clenched. "You're wrong. You're making it up."

"Am not. What's your problem?"

"He comes around because he's the sheriff, and he's looking out for us. That's it. You take it back."

He might have, but the martial glint in Connor's eyes sparked one in his own. "Get real. Anybody can see Devin's got the hots for your mom."

Connor was on him like a leech, knocking Bryan back, rolling over the dirt. Surprise and panic gave him the first advantage as his fists pummeled at Bryan's ribs. But it was his first fight, and Bryan was a veteran.

Within a few sweaty moments, Bryan had Connor pinned. Both of them were scraped and filthy and breathing hard. In reflex, Bryan bloodied Connor's lip, snarling like a young wolf. "Give up?"

"No." Connor jabbed an elbow out and had Bryan grunting. Into the brambles they rolled, gasping out threats and curses.

Again Bryan pinned him, and again he raised his fist. He stopped, froze. He would have sworn he heard something, something that sounded like a man dying, but it didn't sound of this world.

"You hear that?"

"Yeah." Connor didn't loosen his grip on Bryan's ripped T-shirt, but his eyes darted left and right. "It didn't sound real, though, it sounded like . . ."

"Ghosts." The word came through Bryan's cold lips. "Jeez, Con. They're really here. It's the two-corporals."

Connor didn't move a muscle. He didn't hear it anymore, just the owls and the rustle of small animals in the brush. But he felt it, and he suddenly understood. That was what war was, he thought, stranger against stranger, brother against brother. Fighting. Killing. Dying.

And he was ashamed, because Bryan was his brother and he'd raised his fist to him. Raised his fist, he thought as tears stung his eyes, as Joe Dolin had done to Mama, and to him.

"I'm sorry." He couldn't stop the tears, just couldn't, not even when Bryan stared down at him. "I'm sorry."

"Hey, it's okay. You hit good." Uncomfortable, he patted Connor's shoulder before he levered himself to his feet. Systematically he tugged aside brambles and picked thorns out of his clothes and flesh. "You just got to work on your guard, is all."

"I don't want to fight. I hate fighting." Connor sat up and curled himself into a ball of misery.

Bryan cast around for something to say. "Man, we're a mess. You're going to have to come up with a good story for how we got our clothes torn and stuff. Maybe we could say we were attacked by wild dogs."

"That's stupid. Nobody'd believe that."

"You come up with one, Con," Bryan coaxed. "You're real good at stories."

Connor sighed, kept his head on his knees. He didn't want to lie. He hated lying as much as he did fighting. But he didn't think he could stand seeing disappointment in his mother's eyes. "We'll say we lost the baseball in the blackberry bushes and got all caught up in the thorns."

It was simple, Bryan decided. And sometimes simple was best. "How about your lip? It's going to puff up real good."

"I guess I fell down."

Bryan wiped his hands on his dirty jeans. "Does it hurt? You can put one of the soda cans on it."

"It's okay."

"Look, Con, I didn't mean anything by what I said. Nothing bad about your mom, I mean. She's great. If I thought somebody was saying something bad about my mom, I'd beat the hell out of them."

"It's okay," Connor said again. "I know you weren't."

"Well, what'd you go at me like that for?"

Calmer now, Connor rested his chin on his knees. "I thought Sheriff MacKade was coming around because he liked me."

"Well, sure he likes you."

"He's coming around for my mother. He's probably been kissing her, and maybe even more. You know?"

Bryan shrugged. "Well, since he's stuck on her . . ."

"Everything's been good. Everything's changed, and it's so great the way it is. We've got the apartment, and Mama's happy, and *he's* locked up. Now everything's going to be ruined. If she marries the sheriff, it'll ruin everything."

"Why? Devin's cool."

"I don't want a father, not ever again." Dark eyes dominated Connor's dirty, tear-streaked face. "He'll take over, and things will change back. He'll start drinking and yelling, and hitting."

"Not Devin."

"That's what happens," Connor said in a fierce whisper. "It'll all be his instead of ours, and it'll all have to be his way. And if it isn't, he'll hurt her and make her cry."

He had an image of Devin making a vow, offering his hand on it, right here in the woods. But he pushed it aside.

"That's what fathers do."

"Mine doesn't," Bryan said reasonably. "He'd never hit my mom. He yells, but she yells back. Sometimes she yells first. It's pretty cool."

"He hasn't hit her yet. She just hasn't made him mad enough."

"She makes him real mad sometimes. One time, she made him so mad I thought smoke was going to come out of his ears, like in a cartoon. He picked her right up and threw her over his shoulder."

"See."

Bryan shook his head. "He didn't hurt her. They started wrestling around on the grass, and she was yelling at him and swearing. Then they started laughing. Then they started kissing." Bryan rolled his eyes. "Man, it was embarrassing."

"If he'd really been mad—"

"I'm telling you, he was. His face gets real hard, and his eyes, too. He was really steaming."

"Did it scare you?"

"Nah." Then Bryan moved his shoulders again. "Well, maybe it does just a little, when I do something to make him really mad at me. But it's not because I think he's going to belt me or anything." Bryan let out a long breath, then shifted so that he could drape an arm over Connor's shoulders. "Look, Con, Devin's not like Joe Dolin."

"He fights."

"Yeah, but not with girls, or kids."

"What's the difference?"

Connor was about the smartest person he knew, Bryan thought, but he could be so dopey. "You just socked me, right? Are you going to go home and whip up on Emma?"

"Of course not. I'd never—" He broke off, brooding. "Maybe it's different. I have to think about it."

"Cool." Satisfied, Bryan rubbed his sore ribs. "Let's break out a soda, and you can make up a ghost story. A really gruesome one."

* * *

Because Devin had awakened early, he was up and feeding the pigs when he spotted the two boys crossing from the woods with their gear and bag of trash. He lifted a hand in greeting, then cocked a brow when he saw the scrapes, bruises and ripped shirts.

"Must have been some night," he said mildly. "Run into bears?"

Bryan chuckled and greeted the exuberant Fred and Ethel. "Nah. Wolves."

"Um-hmm..." He studied Connor's puffy lip. "Looks like you put up a hell of a battle." He started to reach out for Connor's chin, but the boy jerked back.

"We lost the baseball in the berry bushes," Connor said flatly. "We got tangled up, and I fell."

"Your mothers'll probably buy that," Devin decided. "Your dad won't," he told Bryan. "But he'll let it slide." He emptied the bucket of grain into the trough and had the pigs squealing greedily. "How'd it go otherwise?"

"It was great." Bryan stepped onto the bottom rung of the fence to watch the pigs. "We ate hot dogs and marshmallows and told ghost stories. We even heard the ghosts."

"Sounds eventful."

"Thank you for the tent," Connor said stiffly.

"No problem. Why don't you hang on to it? I imagine you'll use it again before I will."

"I don't want it," Connor said, with a lack of courtesy so out of character, Devin only stared. "I don't want anything." He dropped the tent on the ground. "I have to go." He stood for a moment, chin jerked up, waiting for Devin to show him what happened when you sassed.

But Devin only studied his face, and there was puzzlement, rather than anger, in his eyes. "Put some ice on that lip."

Shoulders stiff, Connor turned and walked quickly away, without a word to his friend.

"I'll keep the tent, Devin." Mortified, and irritated, Bryan shot Connor's back a seething look. "He doesn't mean to be a jerk."

"He's ticked at me. Do you know why?" When Bryan kept his head down, his hands in his pockets, Devin sighed. "I don't want you to break a confidence, Bry. If I've done something to hurt Connor, I'd like to make it right."

"I guess it's my fault." Miserable, Bryan scuffed his shoe in the dirt. "I said something about how you were stuck on his mom, and he went nutso."

Devin rubbed a hand over his suddenly tensed neck. "Is that what you fought about?" No answer again, and Devin nodded. "Okay. Thanks for telling me."

"Devin." Loyalty had never been a problem for Bryan before. Now he felt himself tugged in different directions. "It's just—he's just scared. I mean, Con's not a wimp or anything, but he's scared that if you have, you know, like a thing going with Mrs. Dolin, things'll be like they were. Before, you know. He's got it stuck in his mind that you'd start punching out on his mom the way that bastard—I mean the way Joe Dolin did." Bryan looked around, but Connor had already disappeared into the woods. "I tried to tell him he was off, but I guess he didn't really believe me.''

"Okay. I got it.''

"He'll probably hate me for telling you.''

"No, he won't. You did right, Bryan. You're a good friend.''

"You're not mad at him, are you, for talking back?''

"No, I'm not mad at him. You know how Jared feels about you, Bryan?''

Pleasure and embarrassment mixed, tinted his cheeks. "Yeah.''

"I feel pretty much the same way about Con, and Emma. I just have to give him time to get used to it.''

She'd tried not to worry. Really she had. But when she looked out the window and saw Connor crossing toward the inn, the relief was huge. Cassie set aside the flour she'd taken out for pancakes and went to the kitchen door of the inn.

"I'm down here, Connor. Did you have—'' She saw the bruised face, the torn clothes, and her heart froze in her chest. She was outside like a bullet, terror seeping out of every pore. "What happened? Oh, baby, who hurt you? Let me—''

"I'm all right.'' Still seething, Connor jerked away from her. The look he aimed at her was one she'd never seen from him before. It was filled with fury and disdain. "I'm just fine. Isn't that what you always told me after he hit you? I fell down, I slipped. I walked into the damn door.''

"Connor.''

"Well, I'll tell you the truth. I had a fight with Bryan. I hit him, he hit me."

"Honey, why would you—"

Again he jerked away from her hands. "It's my business why. I don't have to tell you everything, just like you don't tell me everything."

It was rare, very rare, for her to have to discipline the boy. "No, you don't," she said evenly. "But you will mind your tone when you speak to me."

His swollen lip trembled, but he kept his eyes steady. "Why didn't you ever tell him that? Why didn't you ever tell him to mind his tone when he spoke to you? You let him say anything he wanted, do anything he wanted."

Her own shame at hearing the bald truth from her son swamped her. "Connor, if this is about your father—"

"Don't call him that. Don't *ever* call him my father. I hate him, and I'm ashamed of you."

She made some sound as tears sprang to her eyes, but she couldn't speak.

"You're going to let it happen again," Connor raged on. "You're just going to let it happen."

"I don't know what you're talking about, Connor. Come inside and sit down and let's straighten this out."

"There's nothing to say. I won't stay if you marry Sheriff MacKade. I won't stay and watch when he hits you. I won't let you make me have a father again."

She sucked in a harsh breath, forced it out again. "I'm not going to marry him, Connor. I'd just started to think about it, but I would never have made a decision on something that important without talking to you and Emma. And I'd never marry anyone if you were against it. I couldn't."

"He wants you to."

"Yes, he wants me to. He loves me and wants us to be a family. He deserves a family." When she said it, she realized how true it was, how selfish she'd been to ask him to wait. "He cares for us. I thought you cared for him, Connor."

"I don't want a father. I'm not ever going to have one, no matter what you do. Everything's good now, and you're going to ruin it."

"No, I won't." She blinked the tears back. "Go upstairs now, Connor, and get cleaned up."

"I won't—"

"Do as you're told," she said sternly. "However you feel about me, I'm your mother and I'm in charge. I have to fix breakfast down here. You clean up and keep an eye on Emma until I'm finished."

She turned and walked back into the kitchen.

Somehow she got through it, the cooking, the serving, the conversations. When she'd finished clearing up, she checked on the children, suggested that they play in the yard while she tidied the guest rooms.

She refused Connor's stiff offer to help, and left them to play. She was changing the linens on the bed in Abigail's room when she heard the front door open and close.

She knew it was Devin. She knew he'd come.

She didn't know that Connor had heard the car and, demanding a vow of silence from Emma, crept into the hallway.

"Can I give you a hand with that?" Devin asked.

"No." Cassie smoothed the contoured sheet out then reached for the top one. "I've got it."

"I saw Con and Bry over at the farm this morning. You're not upset with him, are you? Boys get into tussles."

"No, I'm not upset about that."

"About what?"

She drew a breath. She'd gone over it in her mind countless times already that morning. She'd let her children down all their lives. Whatever it cost, she would never do so again.

"Devin, I need to talk to you."

"I'm here."

"Connor's very upset, very hurt." She kept her hands busy, tucking the sheet, folding it down, smoothing it. "He's sensed, or been told, something about us, and—"

"I know. I told you I saw him this morning. I'd say what he is, Cassie, is mad."

"Yes, he is. And upset, and hurt. Frightened," she added, pressing her lips together to steady them. "Most of all, frightened. I can't let him be frightened, Devin. Not after what he's already been through."

"You didn't cause it."

"Didn't I?" Meticulously she fluffed and patted the pillows into place. "Doing nothing to stop it all those years is the same as causing it. The first eight years of his life were a nightmare I didn't put an end to. I thought I was shielding him. I told myself I was. But he knew. He's ashamed of me."

"That's not true, Cassie." Devin moved to her, took her hands. "If he said that, it was because he was angry with me, and you were the nearest target. He adores you."

"I've hurt him, Devin, more than I ever realized. Maybe Emma, too. I see now that I've just started to make things right, make things up to them. Now I'm letting it change before they can adjust, before they can trust. I can't do that, Devin. And I can't see you anymore."

Panic reared up, echoed clearly in his voice. "You know that's not the answer. I'll talk to him."

"I don't want you to do that." Cassie tugged her hands from his. "I have to handle this, Devin. I need to prove to Connor that I can, and that he and Emma come first."

"I'm not asking to come ahead of them, damn it, just to be a part of your life. Of their lives. I love you, Cassie."

"I know. I love you. I always will. But I can't be with you. Don't ask me to choose."

"What are you asking me to do?" he demanded. "To just walk away? I've waited for you for twelve years. I can't keep waiting for everything to be perfect. It's never going to be perfect, it just has to be right. We're right, Cassie. You mean everything to me. So do the kids. I need you. I need all of you."

That cut her heart out. "Devin, if things were different—"

"We'll make them different," he insisted, taking her by the shoulders. "We'll make it work."

"I'm not going to ask you to wait." She stepped back, turned toward the window. "You need me, and hearing you say that is wonderful, even more wonderful than when you first told me you loved me. But Connor needs me, too. And he's just a little boy. He's my little boy, and he's frightened."

She took a deep breath, so that she could get it all out cleanly. "You want marriage, family, and you're entitled to that. You're entitled to have someone who's free to give you what you want and need. But I'm not free, and I may never be free. I can't give you what you're entitled to, so I can't be with you, Devin."

"You expect me just to step back, as if nothing's happened between us? Just step back and wait?"

"No. It's time you stopped waiting."

"There's no one but you."

Her heart ripped in two ragged pieces—one for the man, one for the boy. "You haven't let there be. I let you hold on to me, Devin. I think part of me always knew you'd be there. And that was so unfair. I'm trying to be fair now, to everyone."

"Fair? It's fair to toss me, all of what we have together, aside, because a ten-year-old boy demands it? When the hell are you going to take charge, Cassie?"

It was the first time he'd ever hurt her. She faced it, accepted it. "That's what I'm trying to do. Taking charge doesn't always mean doing what you want. Sometimes it means doing what's right for the people you love."

"Damned if I'll beg you." Suddenly bitter, suddenly furious, he bit off each word. "Damned if I'll ask you again, Cassie. I've had enough of standing on the sidelines and breaking my heart over you. I've stripped myself bare for the last time.''

''Hurting you is the last thing I want, Devin. But I can't give you what you need most, so I can't give you anything.''

His eyes cut into her, as hard and searing as his voice. ''It's time it was down to all or nothing. You've made your choice. Looks like I've made mine.''

She listened to his receding footsteps, heard the door slam downstairs. This, she knew, was what Abigail had felt when she sent the man she loved away. This emptiness, this emptiness that was too huge for grief.

Cassie sat on the edge of the bed, buried her face in her hands, and sobbed.

In the corner of the hallway, Connor kept his hand tight on his sister's.

''Mama's crying,'' Emma whispered.

''I know.'' It wasn't Joe Dolin that had made her cry either, Connor thought. And it wasn't Sheriff MacKade.

It was him, and only him.

While Cassie wept and Connor crept downstairs with grief and guilt heavy on his shoulders, Joe Dolin took his chance. He'd waited, oh, he'd waited so patiently, for just the right moment.

The creek rushed under the Burnside Bridge with a harsh bubbling sound. The trees were thick with leaves. His supervisor was gesturing to one of the other men, his attention distracted by a nest of copperheads they'd unearthed.

That was all it took.

Joe bent to gather litter, working his way toward cover, step by careful step. And then he melted into the trees. As he walked quickly through the woods he stripped off his orange vest and tossed it into the brush beside the creek.

He didn't run, not right away. He still had trouble with the peripheral vision in his right eye, thanks to an injury he'd received when he attacked Regan Mac-Kade. So he moved carefully at first, deliberately turning his head to judge his ground, and his distance.

Then he sprinted, wild as a dog, over rocks, through brush, and finally into the creek. Breathing hard, he kept to the water, following its curves and angles. Before long, he was wet to the waist, but he kept going, pushing himself.

Panting, he scrambled up the side of the bank, using rocks and vines to heave himself clear. Then he took a deep gulp of freedom. He would use the sun, and the direction of the creek, to show him the way he wanted to go.

When Devin made up his mind, he was as hard to swerve as a six-ton truck. So when Rafe wandered into his office, saw Devin sitting behind his desk, typing furiously with his face set in stubborn lines, he knew there was trouble.

"I'm supposed to ask you to dinner," Rafe said easily.

"Beat it."

"Regan wanted to have the whole family over tomorrow, plus Cassie and the kids."

"I'm going to be busy. Now get the hell out of here."

"I didn't mention what time," Rafe continued, and walked over to look over Devin's shoulder. "What the hell's this?"

"Just what it looks like."

"Looks like a resignation to me. What wild hair do you have up your—?"

"Get off my back."

Rafe did the brotherly thing and ripped the paper out of the typewriter. "Chill out." Before Devin could lunge to his feet, Rafe slapped a hand on his shoulder. "Look, we can pound each other, I don't mind, but why don't we get the preliminaries out of the way? What the hell are you doing resigning as sheriff?"

"What I should have done a long time ago. I'm getting the hell out of this town. I'm tired of being stuck here in the same damn rut, with the same damn people."

"Dev, you like nothing better than a rut." Rafe tossed the paper aside. "What happened with Cassie?"

"Nothing. Leave it."

"Aren't you the one who came breathing down my neck and made me face up to what I felt for Regan? One good turn."

"I don't have to face what I feel for Cassie. I've faced it for years. What I have to do is get over it."

"She turn you down?" The vicious gleam in Devin's eyes didn't frighten Rafe; it touched him. "Go ahead, take a shot at me. I'll give you a free one."

"Forget it." Deflated, Devin dropped back into his chair.

"Want to talk about it?"

"I'm talked out." He rubbed his hands over his face. "I'm tired. Connor doesn't trust me, she doesn't trust me. It comes down to neither of them wanting me enough. I can't keep trying to prove myself."

"The kid's come a long way, Dev. So has Cassie. Give them a little time."

"I've run out of time. I need something back, Rafe." Devin drew a deep breath. "I just can't keep hurting like this. It's killing me. I'm getting out."

Before Rafe could speak, the phone rang. Devin snagged the receiver and all but spit into it, "Sheriff's office. MacKade." He was on his feet in a flash, swearing violently. "When? That's over a damn hour ago. Why in hell wasn't I notified? Don't give me that crap." He listened for another minute, then slammed down the receiver.

"Dolin's out." He strode over to the gun cabinet, unlocked it and pulled out a rifle. "You're deputized."

Chapter 12

Joe stayed hunkered in the ravine across from the little rancher where his mother-in-law lived. He doubted they'd look for him there, not right away. They'd go to his friends, check on Cassie. Maybe, just maybe, MacKade or one of his horse-faced deputies would swing by.

But his mama-in-law wasn't home. There was no car in the drive, and the curtains were drawn tight over the front windows.

The ranch house sat on the edge of a dead-end road, and was perfect for his purposes. He kept his eyes peeled, then scurried out of the ravine, keeping low. The far side of the house faced nothing but trees, so he used that for his entry. With an elbow, he shattered a window.

Once inside, he headed toward the main bedroom. He needed fresh clothes, and knew she kept some of her dead husband's things hanging in the closet like shrouds.

The old bag was morbid.

She was also paranoid.

That was how he knew there would be a pistol in her nightstand drawer, fully loaded. The only thing he wouldn't find in the house was a drink. But he'd see to that soon enough.

Instead, in dry clothes too small for his frame, he settled down to wait.

He heard her drive up, listened to her fiddling with the locks and bolts on the front door. He smiled as he rose and walked out into the darkened living room.

She was carrying a bag of groceries in one arm, a cheap purse in the other. Her eyes widened when she saw him.

"Joe, what in the world—"

He did what he'd wanted to do for years. He swung out and knocked her flat with the back of his hand.

Actually, he thought about killing her. But he wanted to save that for his darling little wife. As she moaned and flailed at him weakly, he tied her with clothesline, gagged her. Once she was secured, wriggling like a fish on the floor, he dumped out her purse.

"Twenty lousy bucks," he complained. "I shoulda known." He stuffed the bills in his pocket and picked up her keys. "I'm going to borrow your car, need to take a little trip. A little trip with my wife. A wife's bound to go where her husband tells her to go, isn't that right?"

He grinned as she rolled her eyes, as sick panic dulled them. "It was real obliging of you to write all those letters to the prison. Real obliging. That's why I'm not going to mess you up too bad. I want to show you how I appreciate it."

He laughed when Constance moaned and babbled against the gag. "Now, Cassie's a different thing, isn't she? She didn't stick by her husband like a proper wife, did she? But I'm going to take care of that. I'm going to teach her a real good lesson. Want to hear what I'm going to do to your daughter, old woman? Want to hear what I got planned for her?"

Because he was enjoying the panic in her eyes, Joe hunkered down and told her.

Devin squealed to a halt at the inn. His eyes scanned every bush, every tree, as he hurried around to the back and up the stairs. He didn't stop praying until he opened the door and saw Cassie at the stove.

He couldn't help it. He grabbed her, dragged her hard against him and just held on.

"Devin—"

"Sorry." Clamping down on every emotion, he drew back and became a cop again. "I have to talk to you." He flicked a glance to the living room, where Connor and Emma sat staring at him. He started to tell Connor to take Emma to her room and stay there, then realized he was thinking like a father, not a cop. "Joe walked off work release just over an hour ago."

Cassie's knees buckled. Devin held her up and guided her to a chair. "Sit down, and listen. I've got people checking on his known associates, the places where he used to hang out. We'll pick him up, Cassie. Does he know you're living here?''

"I don't know," she said dully. "My mother might have— I don't know.''

"We won't chance it. I want you to get whatever you need. I'm going to take you over to the cabin.''

"The cabin?''

"You'll stay with Savannah. I need Jared. I need Shane, too, or I'd have taken you over to the farm. Pull it together, Cassandra,'' he said, sharply enough to have her eyes clearing.

"I can't go to the cabin, Devin. I can't put Savannah and her children in danger.''

"Savannah can handle it.''

"So can I. Give me a minute.'' She needed to take a breath. "Connor and Emma will go wherever you think they'll be safe.''

"No, ma'am.'' Connor curled his trembling hand over Emma's. "I'm not going anywhere without you. I'm not leaving you.''

"Nobody's leaving anybody. You're all going where I tell you to go. Get your things,'' Devin snapped. "Or do without them.''

"Savannah is not responsible for me and mine,'' Cassie said slowly. "I am.''

"I don't have the time to be patient with you. I can't stay here and take care of you, so you're going.''

He whirled around. Connor, his stomach queasy, saw a kind of fury he'd never seen before, not even in Joe Dolin's eyes. "Get downstairs, into the car.''

"I can take care of my mother.''

"I'm counting on it, but not here. Do as I tell you, Connor.''

"Devin, take the children, and—"

"The hell with this." He spun around again, picked Cassie up bodily and flung her over his shoulder. "Out!" he shouted at Connor, then swore when the boy's blood drained out of his face. "Damn it, boy, don't you see I'd die before I'd hurt her? Before I'd hurt any of you?"

And Connor did, so clearly that the shame of it burned color back into his cheeks. "Yes, sir. Come on, Emma."

"Put me down, Devin." Cassie didn't bother to struggle. "Please, put me down. We'll go."

He set her on her feet, keeping his hands on her shoulders for a moment. "You have to let me take care of you. You have to let me do that, at least. Trust me, Cassie."

"I do." She reached for Connor's hand. "We do."

"Make it quick." He put a hand on the screen door, scanned quickly before stepping out. "We've got roadblocks," he began. "Helicopters are on the way. Odds are we'll have him before nightfall. How many at the inn?"

"No one. We have a family coming in tonight, but—"

"I'll take care of it. Just don't—"

When the shot rang out, it was so sudden, so shocking, Cassie could do nothing but gasp. Devin collapsed at her feet.

"Hi, honey." Joe walked forward, a grin on his face, a gun in his hand. "I'm home."

She did the only thing she could do. She shoved the children behind her and faced him.

She saw the changes in him. His face was thinner, harder, as his body was. There was a scar beside and beneath his right eye, puckered and white. But the eyes themselves were the same. Brutal.

"I'll go with you, Joe." She knew Devin was breathing, but there was blood on his temple where the bullet had streaked. He needed help, an ambulance. The only way to save him and her children was to surrender herself. "I'll go wherever you want. Just don't hurt my babies."

"I'll do whatever I want with your brats, bitch. And you'll do just what I tell you." He looked down at Devin, sneered. "Not so tough now, is he? I should have aimed better." He squinted, laughed. "Got a little problem with the eye, but I'll do a lot better close up."

As if in a dream, she saw his face, saw the gun lower. The cold came over her, the cold and the knowledge that this had happened before. Only then it had been a young, wounded soldier and a woman too weak, too frightened, to save him.

"No!" She screamed, threw herself over Devin's body. "He's hurt!" She knew those words were useless, and struggled to find others. "If you kill him, Joe, and they catch you, you'll never get out again. Do you know what happens when you kill a police officer? It isn't worth it. I said I'd go with you."

"You stay there, I'll just shoot through you. Then, maybe..." He smiled again, shifted his gun toward Connor.

"Stay away from my babies!" Like a woman possessed, she lunged, threw herself at him with a fire and fury that nearly knocked him over. Even when he hit her, she clung like a burr. Then Connor was on him, pummeling, shouting.

Joe swatted him off like a fly.

"I'll teach you manners, you little brat." Before he could strike out with the butt of the gun, he heard the sound of sirens. "Later," he said as Connor scrambled to his feet. "I'll be back for you later." He had am arm around Cassie's throat, choking her, the gun to her temple.

His only escape, he saw, was the woods. "I'll kill her!" he shouted to anyone who could hear. "Anyone comes after me, she's dead!"

He dragged her away, trampling flowers.

On the ground, Emma squeezed Devin's hand. "Please wake up. Please wake up."

Connor crawled to him as Rafe and a deputy rushed around the house. "He shot him, he shot him and he took Mama!"

Grim-faced, Rafe bent over his brother. "It's not as bad as it looks." It helped to say it. He pulled a bandana out of his pocket and stanched the blood. "He's coming around," he murmured, and relief washed through him in a flood as Devin stirred. "Connor, go in and call an ambulance. Hurry."

"No." Devin's eyes fluttered open. He batted his brother's hand away. "I'm okay. Cassie—"

"You're shot, you idiot." But even as Rafe tried to hold him down, Devin was fighting his way up.

His vision wavered, grayed. A short stream of oaths helped steady it again. "Where'd he take her?"

"To the woods." Connor bit his lip. "He took her into the woods. He was hurting her. I tried to stop him."

"Take care of your sister," Devin ordered. "I want men posted around the woods. Notify Jared, tell him to get back to the cabin. He might go there. You stay with these kids," he ordered his deputy. "Get them inside."

"I'm going in with you," Rafe stated.

"You can go in." Eyes cold, Devin drew his weapon. "But he's mine."

Cassie did whatever she could to slow him down now that he was away from her children and Devin. She would not be a silent victim again. She scratched, she bit, she kicked.

"Forgot who's boss, didn't you? Thought you could lock me up in a cage and forget who was in charge." Cursing her, he shoved the gun into his waistband, so that he could use both hands to drag her. "I'm going to have a good time reminding you."

"They'll find you. They'll catch you and lock you up for good this time."

"Maybe they'll catch me, maybe they won't." He stumbled along, hauling her after him and losing his direction in his fury. He hated these damn woods, the MacKade woods. "I've had a lot of time to think about this. I know just what we're going to do. We're going to get us a car. That's what we're going to do."

He cursed the fact that he'd had to leave the one he'd already stolen behind.

"I've got friends," he muttered. "I've got plenty of friends who'll help me out."

"You've got no one. You never did. Devin'll come after you, Joe, and he'll never stop."

"He's lying on his back and bleeding to death."

"He'll never stop," she said again. "Nothing you do to me will come close to what he'll do to you."

"Got something going with him, don't you?" Joe stopped, breathless, and dragged her head back by the hair. He thought he heard voices in his head, voices saying the words just before he did. "You whore. I own you. Don't you forget it. I own you. Till death do us part."

"You're a miserable, drunken bully." Defiance bolted through her like lightning. "You don't own anything, not even yourself. You're pathetic." She barely winced when he yanked mercilessly on her hair. "The only thing you can beat is something weaker than you. Go ahead, Joe, hit me. It's the only thing you know how to do. But this time, damn you to hell, you're in for a fight."

He released her hair, using that hand to knock her sprawling on the path. The pain only energized her. Eyes hot and deadly, she got to her feet, her fists clenched.

He stepped forward, and she braced, ready, even eager, to defend herself.

"If you touch her, if you breathe on her, I'll put a hole in you."

Slowly Joe turned. Devin was less than three yards back on the path, his weapon drawn and aimed. Rafe MacKade was behind him. As his eyes darted in search of an escape, Shane stepped out of the trees. And Jared moved up the path behind Cassie.

"Drop the gun, Dolin, take it out slow and drop it, or I'll kill you."

"You're plenty brave, MacKade." Joe wet his lips as he took the gun out with two fingers, stooped to set it on the ground. "When you've got four guns on me, and your brothers standing by."

"Kick it this way."

"Yeah, a real hero, long as it's not one-to-one." Joe gave the gun a shove with his foot. "You've been helping yourself to my wife, haven't you?"

"You don't have a wife." Devin turned, handed his gun to Rafe. "Stay back," he demanded, then skimmed a glance over his other brothers. "All of you." He looked at Cassie briefly, saw the bruises already forming. And felt hatred wash through him. "Get to the cabin, Cassie. Savannah will take you back to the kids."

"You don't have to do this."

"Oh, yeah. I do." And he smiled. "Let's go, Joe. It's been a long time coming."

"What's to stop one of your brothers from shooting me in the back once I beat you to a pulp, Mac-Kade?"

"Nothing." Now the smile turned feral. "This is the last shot you're going to get at me, though, you yellow son of a bitch. So make it good."

Joe shouted ferociously as he lunged. All Devin had to do was pivot and pump upward with a fist to send Joe reeling back.

"Tougher when it's somebody near your own size, isn't it?" Devin taunted. "Tougher when it's not a woman, or a little boy. Come on, you bastard. Try again."

Blood spilling from his lip, Joe came at him like a bull. The woods cracked with the sound of bare knuckle against bone, of men grunting. Cassie forced herself not to cover her face with her hands.

It was for her. Each blow Devin threw or received was for her. So she would watch.

All the fear she'd felt of Joe ebbed as she did. He was exactly what she had called him. A pitiful bully. His size, and the wildness of his attack, helped him land a few blows. Certainly, it was that size that had him overbalancing Devin to the ground.

But even there, even outweighed, Devin dominated. His fists were fast, brutal, and the look on his face was so concentrated, she knew he felt none of the hits he took.

She didn't turn her face away from the blood, hold her hands over her ears to block out the sound. This was the end, finally the end, and she needed to bear witness.

The rage was on him so thick, so cold, that he could see nothing but Joe's face. Each time his fist hammered down, each time the power of it sang up his arms, he felt nothing but dark, deadly pleasure. His knuckles were raw, his shirt was splattered with blood, some of it his own, but he couldn't stop his fist from pumping.

"That's enough." Jared stepped forward to pull Devin off, and nearly got a fist in the face for his trouble. "That's enough," he repeated, but it took all three of them to drag Devin to his feet.

"That's a satisfying sight," Rafe commented, studying Joe's battered and unconscious face. "I guess I can't be too ticked you didn't leave a piece of him for me."

"Looks like he resisted arrest, right, Jare?" Shane shouldered his rifle, scratched his chin.

"That's the way I saw it. Come on, Dev, let's haul this carcass in. You need a beer and an ice pack."

But the rage hadn't faded away, not completely. Devin jerked his brother's hand from his shoulder. "Leave me alone." He turned, looked to where Cassie still stood, pale, bruised, eyes wide with shock. "I'm finished." He took off his badge, tossed it into the dirt. "Take him. I'm going home."

"Devin."

When Cassie started forward, Jared put out a hand to stop her. "Give him some time," he murmured, watching Devin cut through the woods, toward the farm. "He's hurting."

She tried. She went to her children and comforted them. She let Regan and Savannah come to her and fuss over her bruises. She spoke to her mother, briefly, on the phone and reassured herself that, though her mother had been bruised and terrified, there was no serious damage. And, perhaps, there was some understanding between them that they'd never shared before.

In the end, she gave in and took the sedative that was pushed on her and slept like the dead through the night.

But in the morning she knew she hadn't finished facing her demons. She let Regan deal with breakfast and readied herself to go to the farm and face Devin.

The only thing she needed to take, she tucked into the pocket of her slacks.

"You're going to see Sheriff MacKade." Connor stepped into her bedroom doorway. His eyes were swollen and shadowed, there was a faint bruise on his cheek, and he was still so very pale. Cassie wanted badly to gather him close, but he was standing so stiff.

"Yes. I need to talk to him, Connor. I need to thank him for what he did."

"He'll say it was his job."

"Yes, I know he will. That doesn't mean I don't have to thank him. He could have been killed, Connor, for us."

"I thought he was dead at first." When his voice broke, he sucked in a breath and steadied it again. "When he fell, and there was all the blood. I thought we were all going to be dead."

She shuddered, tried to keep the tears out of her voice. "I'm sorry, Connor, for what I did, for what I didn't do. I hope one day you'll forgive me."

"It wasn't your fault. It wasn't ever. I shouldn't have said those things." He wanted to look away, but he knew that would make him a coward. He knew what cowards were like now. "It wasn't true, and it wasn't the way I really felt. I said it to hurt you, because I felt bad."

"Connor." She held her arms out, closing her eyes tight when he raced into them. "That part of our lives is over. I promise you it's over."

"I know. You were pretty brave."

Unbearably touched, she kissed the top of his head. "So were you."

"This time." He sucked in a deep breath. "Sheriff MacKade stood up for us. Emma and I want to go with you. We talked about it. We want to see the sheriff."

"It might be better if I talked to him alone, just now. He's feeling . . . He's upset."

"I have to talk to him. Please."

How could she deny her child the same closure she needed for herself? "All right. We'll go together."

From his seat on the front porch of the farm, Devin saw them come out of the woods. He nearly got up and went inside, but it seemed a small and petty revenge.

They looked like a unit, he realized, and he supposed, however much it hurt him, that was what they needed to be.

His head was still aching, and his hands burned. But that was nothing compared to the pain in his gut as he watched Cassie and the children cross the wide front lawn.

There were bruises on her face, and on the boy's. Fury flashed in his blood like lightning. Then Emma broke away from Cassie's hand and raced to him.

"We came to thank you because you took the bad man away." She crawled right into his lap, as if she belonged there. "You have hurts." Solemnly she touched her puckered lips to the cuts and bruises, to the white bandage on his temple. "Is that better now?"

He gave in for a moment and pressed his face into her hair. "Yeah, thanks." Before Cassie could speak, he shifted Emma onto his knee. "If they haven't contacted you, I can tell you they've already transferred him to the state prison. With the new charges—the escape, the assaults, grand theft auto, the weapons possession, assault with a deadly weapon and—" he ran his fingers over his ripped knuckles "—and resisting arrest, he's not going to see the light of day again. You and your family have nothing to worry about."

"Are you all right?" was all Cassie could manage.

"I'm fine. You?"

"Just fine." Her fingers curled and uncurled over Connor's. "We wanted to come and thank—"

"I was doing my job."

"I told her you'd say that," Connor said, and earned a mild glance from Devin.

"So, I'm predictable." He looked back at Cassie. "You handled yourself well, Cass. You want to remember that. I've got work to do."

As he started to set Emma down, Cassie moved forward. "Devin, please, don't."

"He hurt you." The words burst out of him. "He hurt all of you, and I didn't stop him."

"You were shot, for God's sake. You were lying there unconscious and bleeding."

"The bad man was going to shoot you again," Emma told him. "But Mama wouldn't let him. She lay on top of you so he couldn't."

Every ounce of his hot blood went cold at the thought of it. "Damn it, Cassie, are you crazy?"

"You needed me." She let out a shaky breath. "I couldn't stand back, Devin. I did what I had to do. Now I'm going to ask you to do what you know is right." She took his badge out of her pocket. "Don't give this up, Devin. Don't go."

He stared at the badge in her hand, then into her face again. "You know what it's like to see something you want, you need, day after day, and know you can't have it? I'm not living like that anymore, not even for you. You won't let me be part of your life.

You won't marry me, and I can't go on being your friend and nothing else.''

"I'll marry you." Emma curled into him. "I love you.''

His heart simply shattered. He held Emma tight, then set her gently on her feet. "I can't handle this, Cassie.'' He rose blindly. "Go home and leave me be.''

"Sheriff MacKade.'' Connor bolted forward, then skidded to a halt. "I'm sorry.''

"You've got a right to your feelings,'' Devin said steadily. "And no need to apologize for them.''

"Sir, I got something to say.''

Devin rubbed a hand over his face, dropped his arms. "All right, get it out, then.''

"I know you're mad at me. Yes, sir, you are,'' Connor said keeping his eyes level when Devin started to correct him. "I was mad, too, because I thought you'd come around just for me, or mostly, and then I found out it was because of Mama. And I thought if she'd let you, you'd change things, and they'd get bad again, even though you'd given your word. Bryan told me they wouldn't, but I didn't believe him. I didn't want to.''

He had to take a deep breath. "Yesterday, when you came to make us go to the cabin, and Mama said she wouldn't, you were mad. You were already mad, and then you were madder than anything. Weren't you?''

"That's right.''

"You yelled.''

"Yeah, I did.''

"I thought this is it, this is when he's going to hit her. You knew I was thinking it, but you weren't going to. You told me you'd never hurt her, not for anything. I knew you meant it. I knew when you went into the woods after her, you'd do anything to save her. It wasn't just because it was your job. It was because it was her. Because it was us.''

He gathered the rest of his shaky courage and climbed the steps until he stood face-to-face with Devin. ''Even after she sent you away, even after I made her send you away, you wouldn't hurt her.''

''I couldn't hurt her, Connor, if my life depended on it. That's how it is.''

''Yes, sir. And she cried.'' He ignored the murmur of protest from his mother and kept his eyes on Devin's. ''After she sent you away, she cried, like she used to when she was hurt and she thought I couldn't hear. But this time I made her cry, and I want to tell you I'm sorry. I want to tell you that I don't want a father. I can't help it.''

''All right.'' Devin knew he would fall apart in a minute. ''It's all right.''

''I don't want a father,'' Connor hurried on. ''Except if he was you.''

The hand Devin had laid on Connor's shoulder tightened painfully. But it was a good, solid feeling, and gave him the boost he needed to finish.

''Please, I want you to be with us all the time, like families are supposed to. I know you might not want me now, after what I did, but I swear I won't get in your way. I was stupid, and I sassed you and Mama, and you can punish me, but don't go away. You don't have to love me anymore, if you'd just—''

The boy's breath whooshed out, along with hot tears as Devin hauled him hard against his chest. ''You're too smart to say stupid things,'' Devin murmured shakily. "I haven't stopped wanting you. I couldn't stop loving you."

"Don't go away." Connor held on for his life. "Please, don't go away and leave us."

"I'm not going anywhere. I'm staying right here, okay?"

"Yes, sir."

"Stop calling me sir all the damn time." He pressed a kiss to Connor's damp brow. Gently he used his thumb to wipe the boy's cheeks as Emma wriggled between them.

"Hold me, too," she demanded. "I want you, too."

So he rose, the girl boosted in one arm, the boy wrapped under the other. Whatever happened now, he had no choice but to follow his heart.

She was standing there, her own eyes swimming, his badge clutched in one hand, the other pressed to her lips.

It wasn't the way he'd pictured it, asking her with two weepy children looking on. But it was going to have to do.

"No one's ever going to love you the way I do, Cassie. No one's ever going to love these children more or work harder to give them a good life. The fact is, I can't live without you, without all of you. You're my heart. For God's sake, Cassie, marry me."

He couldn't know what it meant to her, to hear those words, to have him say them, so simply, so plainly, while he held the children as if they were already his.

Of course, they were. How foolish she'd been to ever think otherwise.

How foolish she'd been to think about doing what Abigail had done, turning away love.

She walked up the steps, took one of Connor's hands, one of Emma's. "You are the most remarkable man I've ever known, and I love you. If you have a fault, it's that you're too patient, Devin."

"I'm running low right now."

"Then I'll make this simple. We've kept you waiting long enough."

She released Connor's hand only long enough to pin the badge back on Devin's shirt. Then, linked again, she lifted to her toes and kissed the man she loved in front of her children.

"We'd love to marry you, Devin. Soon." She laid her head on his heart. "I think all of us have waited long enough. Very, very soon."

* * * * *

Coming in April in Silhouette Special Edition, look for The Fall of Shane MacKade. *Turn the page for a sneak preview....*

A Sneak Preview of

THE FALL OF SHANE MACKADE

Nora Roberts

Silhouette Special Edition
April 1996

As he worked alongside his three brothers, hauling hay to the barn, Devin told himself it wasn't his business. He was used to women falling for Shane, but it was easy to see Rebecca was different. He doubted she'd walk away unscathed when the time came.

They worked together in silence until Shane shut off the motor and squinted up at the sky. "It's going to rain. We haven't got much time to get this in." But his gaze wandered to the house, where Rebecca and the other women were busy in the kitchen.

"Damn it, Shane." Disgusted, Devin pulled out a bandanna and mopped his brow. "You're sleeping with her."

"Who?"

"Don't give me that. Aren't there enough women to

dangle after around here without sniffing around Regan's friend? She's not even your type.''

Shane worked to keep his anger in check. ''You've always said I didn't have a type.''

''You know what I mean. That's a serious woman. Serious women have serious feelings. If she's not in love with you already, she will be. Then what the hell are you going to do?''

''That's my business, isn't it? Mine and Rebecca's. I didn't push her into anything.''

He wasn't going to talk about it, and he certainly wasn't going to worry about it.

A man was entitled to a private life.

''How's it going otherwise?'' Jared asked, with a vague thought to defuse an argument. Rain was beginning to patter the ground, and they had work to do. ''Hasn't been a woman living in the house since Mom died. Cramping your style?''

A smile curved Shane's lips. ''Nope.''

Catching the look, Rafe set down the bale he'd just lifted. ''You *are* sleeping with her.''

''What am I, wearing a sign?''

''Can't you keep it in your pants for once?'' In disgust, Rafe sliced his baling hook down. ''Regan feels responsible for her.''

''Why the hell should anybody feel responsible? She's a grown woman.'' Shane spared Devin a glance before he turned on Rafe. ''It's none of his business, it's none of your business.''

''Anything connected to Regan's my business. And Rebecca's connected. What do you know about her? Do you know how she was brought up? How she spent all her time in classrooms, with tutors, in boarding schools?''

''What difference does it make?'' Irritated because he didn't know—because what he knew was far from enough—Shane ignored the rain, the work, and let out his frustration on his brother. ''She's got a brain, she uses it.''

''That's all she was ever allowed to use. She wouldn't stand a chance if you aimed for her.''

''Back off,'' Shane snarled at Rafe. ''And stay out of my personal life.''

Devin plucked out a spear of hay and gnawed on it. ''We should've figured he'd hit on her.''

''I didn't hit on her.''

''That's bull. She'd barely unpacked her bags and you were stalking her in my kitchen. I should've punched you out right then.''

Shane's eyes narrowed. ''Try it now. You've got it all figured out, don't you? Now that you've got your pretty wife and pretty kids. All of you.'' There was more anger than he'd realized boiling inside of him. ''I live my life my way, not yours. So stick your advice and your judgments and anything else you've got up your—''

From the kitchen window, Rebecca watched the four men. She was puzzled. At first it had seemed they were having some sort of serious discussion. Then it had looked as though an argument was brewing.

''Something's going on out there,'' she commented, and Savannah, an infant over her shoulder, wandered to the window.

''Oh, they're going to go at it.''

''At what?''

"Each other, what else?" She shook her head and called to Regan and Cassie, who were busy at the stove. "Our boys are about to rumble."

"Fight?" Shocked to the core, Rebecca goggled. "You mean they're going to fight with each other? But why?"

Regan walked to the kitchen door, opened it. "It's just something they like to do from time to time."

"Do you think it's soon enough to stop it?" Cassie wondered.

"We can— No," Regan finished as the first blow was launched. "Too late."

With horrified eyes, Rebecca watched Shane's fist streak out and plow into Rafe's face. An instant later, they were rolling in the dirt.

"Why doesn't somebody stop them?" Rebecca demanded. "Jared and Devin are just standing there."

"Not for long," Savannah predicted.

As if on cue, Devin reached down. If his intention was to break it up, he failed miserably. Now there were three men wrestling in the mud the rain had churned up.

"This is ridiculous." By the time Rebecca reached the kitchen door, Jared had joined the fray. "I'm going to put a stop to this thing, right now."

As Rebecca marched out, Savannah slanted a look at Regan. "She's really stuck on him, isn't she?"

"I'm afraid so. It worries me."

"I think she's good for him." Cassie joined them at the door. "I think he's good for her, too. Both of them need someone, even if they haven't figured that out yet."

The only thing Rebecca figured as she marched toward the barn was that these four grown men— brothers, no less—were absolute fools.

By the time Rebecca neared the battlefield, she was soaked. "Stop it."

She stood, hands on hips and realized they were laughing. Four baboons, she decided, laughing while they beat on each other. "Get up from there, all of you. You should be ashamed." Eyes hot, she scalded every one of them in turn. "I said get up. You." Choosing at random, she pointed a righteous finger at Devin. "You're a sheriff, for God's sake. You're supposed to uphold order, and here you are rolling in the mud like a hooligan."

"Yes, ma'am." Gamely Devin swallowed a chuckle and disengaged himself from the tangle of limbs. "Don't know what got into me."

"And you." The valiant finger was aimed at Jared. "A lawyer. What are you thinking of?"

"Nothing." He rubbed a hand over his sore jaw before he rose. "Absolutely nothing."

"Rafe MacKade." She had the pleasure of seeing him wince. "A businessman, a member of the community. Husband and father. What kind of example are you setting for your children?"

"A poor one." He cleared his throat and got to his feet. He had the feeling that if he let the laugh loose, she'd put him on his butt again.

"And you," she said, with such contempt in her voice, Shane decided to stay in the mud. "I thought better of you."

"I didn't start it."

"Typical response. Just typical. Is this how you settle your disagreements? Violence is never the answer, and there's no problem that can't be solved with reason and communication."

"Isn't she something?" Shane said, in a tone that had all three of his brothers studying him. "Have you ever seen anybody like her? Come on and kiss me, sweetie."

"If you think you can—" She let out a shriek as he caught her just at the back of the knees and had her sprawling on top of him. "You idiot! You brainless—"

Then she was flat on her back, covered by wet, hard male. His mouth, trembling with laughter, swooped down on hers. "She's the prettiest little thing."

And then he was kissing her senseless. The rain beat down, mud slicked her hands, and there was an audience of fascinated onlookers.

She just didn't care.

As he watched, Rafe found himself grinning. "I'm damned," he murmured. "She's hooked him."

"I think you're right." Devin rubbed his bloody cheek on his muddy shoulder. "I've never seen him look at any woman that way. Think he knows it?"

"I don't think either of them have a clue." Delighted, Jared swiped wet hair out of his eyes.

"It's going to be a pleasure." Rafe hooked his thumbs in his pockets and rocked back on his heels. "A real pleasure, to watch Shane MacKade take the fall."

∇INTIMATE MOMENTS®

TM *Silhouette*®

COMING NEXT MONTH

#703 SURVIVE THE NIGHT—Marilyn Pappano
Heartbreakers

Framed! Escaped convict Dillon Boone had no choice but to do the unthinkable: take Ashley Benedict hostage. Her home provided a place to heal his wounds, while her arms promised love and acceptance…if only they could survive the night.

#704 DRIVEN TO DISTRACTION—Judith Duncan
Romantic Traditions

If anything, Maggie Burrows's life was pretty darn sedate. Then Toni Parnelli moved in next door—and immediately put the moves on Maggie. He was a younger man, determined to break all the rules—and more than determined to break down Maggie's reserve.

#705 A COWBOY'S HEART—Doreen Roberts

Sharon Douglass had loved and been left by her cowboy, and now their son wanted to follow in the footsteps of his rodeo-riding father…a father he didn't even know. Then Mac McAllister returned to Sharon's ranch expecting to save the day—but instead he got the shock of his life….

#706 BABY OF THE BRIDE—Kay David

Rachel St. James found herself the proud *almost*-mom of a beautiful baby girl—but with no husband in sight! Desperate for the adoption to go through, she proposed nick-of-time nuptials to friend Paul Delaney. Now the last thing the convenient groom wanted was for their marriage to end….

#707 BLACKWOOD'S WOMAN—Beverly Barton
The Protectors

Though Joanna Beaumont had learned the hard way about life's darker side, she still was every bit the romantic. Especially when it came to cynical J. T. Blackwood. His harsh demeanor beckoned her to heal his wounds—even as she welcomed his tender protection from the terror of her past.

#708 AN HONORABLE MAN—Margaret Watson

She'd ruined his life two years ago, and now Julia Carleton had the audacity to ask for his help. Well, ex-cop Luke McKinley would just have to say *no*. Only he couldn't. Not when his silence could mean harming innocent people…or the woman he'd fallen for, despite the odds.

MILLION DOLLAR SWEEPSTAKES

As seen on TV!
Free Gift Offer

With a Free Gift proof-of-purchase from any Silhouette® book,
you can receive a beautiful cubic zirconia pendant.

This gorgeous marquise-shaped stone is a genuine cubic
zirconia—accented by an 18" gold tone necklace.

(Approximate retail value $19.95)

Send for yours today...

compliments of **Silhouette®**

Free Gift Certificate

Name: _____

Address: _____

City: _____ State/Province: _____ Zip/Postal Code: _____

FREE GIFT OFFER   079-KBZ-R
ONE PROOF-OF-PURCHASE

To collect your fabulous FREE GIFT, a cubic zirconia pendant, you must include this original proof-of-purchase for each gift with the properly completed Free Gift Certificate.

079-KBZ-R

If you are looking for more titles by

NORA ROBERTS

Don't miss this chance to order additional stories by
one of Silhouette's favorite authors:

You're About to Become a

Privileged Woman

Reap the rewards of fabulous free gifts and benefits with proofs-of-purchase from Silhouette and Harlequin books

Pages & Privileges™

It's our way of thanking you for buying our books at your favorite retail stores.

✂

```
┌ ─ ─ ─ ─ ─ ─ ─ ─ ─ ─ ─ ─ ┐
│  📖   PROOF OF        │ SIM-PP114
│       PURCHASE        │
│ Offer expires October 31, 1996 │
└ ─ ─ ─ ─ ─ ─ ─ ─ ─ ─ ─ ─ ┘
```

**Harlequin and Silhouette—
the most privileged readers in the world!**

For more information about Harlequin and Silhouette's PAGES & PRIVILEGES program call the Pages & Privileges Benefits Desk: 1-503-794-2499

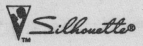

SIM-PP114